KAZUMA KAMACHI

ILLUSTRATION BY
KIYOTAKA HAIMURA

1

CHAPTER 1: THOSE SEEKING RICHES AND ~~LES~~
THIRD FRIDAY OF JANUARY

CW00346006

Member of
Skill-Out
**Shiage
Hamazura**

Boss of
Skill-Out,
an armed
group
made up
of Level
Zeroes
**Ritoku
Komaba**

Member of
Skill-Out
Hanzou

*A
Certain
Magical
Index
SS*

Apprentice Scandinavian warrior maiden **Valkyrie**

English Puritan sorcerer from Necessarius **Kaori Kanzaki**

Italian souvenir-selling girl **Balbina**

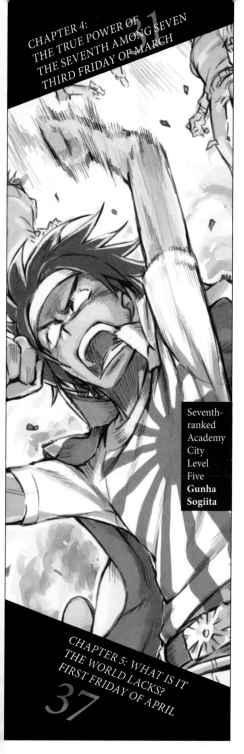

Seventh-
ranked
Academy
City
Level
Five
**Gunha
Sogiita**

Owner of a
Tokiwadai
Middle
School
salon
**Michibata
Sakashima**

Level
Four from
Tokiwadai
Middle
School
**Kuroko
Shirai**

Ollerus's fearsome partner **Sylvia**

Way too helpful of a helper **Ollerus**

Kunoichi girl and self-professed descendant of ninjas **Kuruwa**

Academy
City
Judgment
member
**Kazari
Uiharu**

Mysterious(?)
consultant
**Tabigake
Misaka**

CHAPTER 13: THE PRECISION OF GROUP FORTUNE-TELLING
FOURTH FRIDAY OF AUGUST

95

Military-use clone girls
Misaka Sisters

Tokiwadai Middle School Level Five
Mikoto Misaka

CHAPTER 14: DANCES OF GATEKEEPERS AND INTRUDERS
THIRD FRIDAY OF SEPTEMBER

101

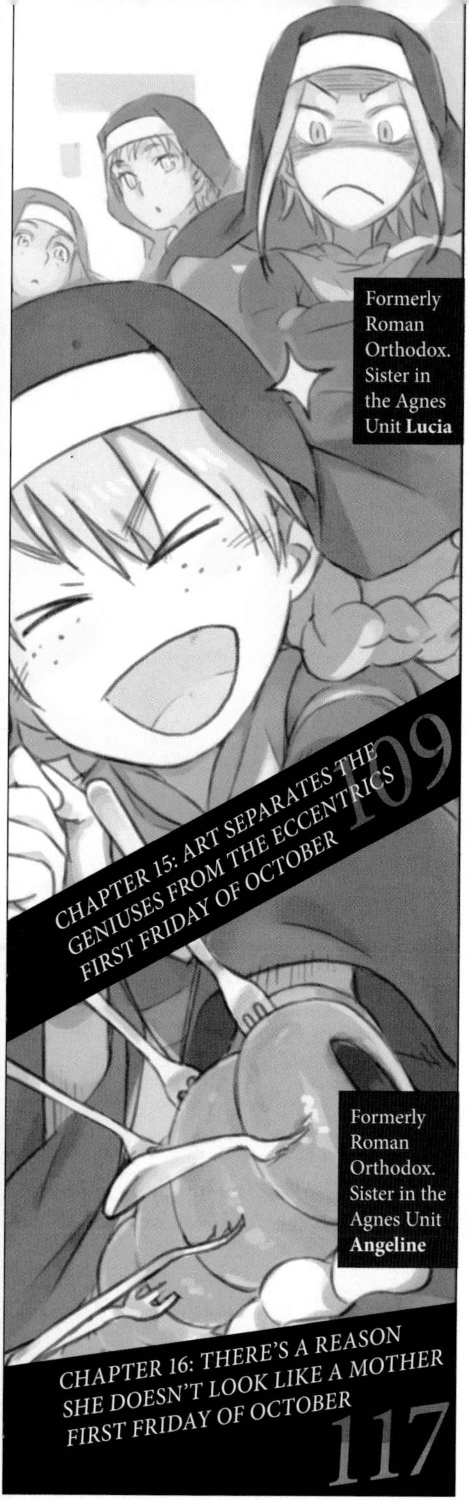
Formerly Roman Orthodox. Sister in the Agnes Unit **Lucia**
Formerly Roman Orthodox. Sister in the Agnes Unit **Angeline**

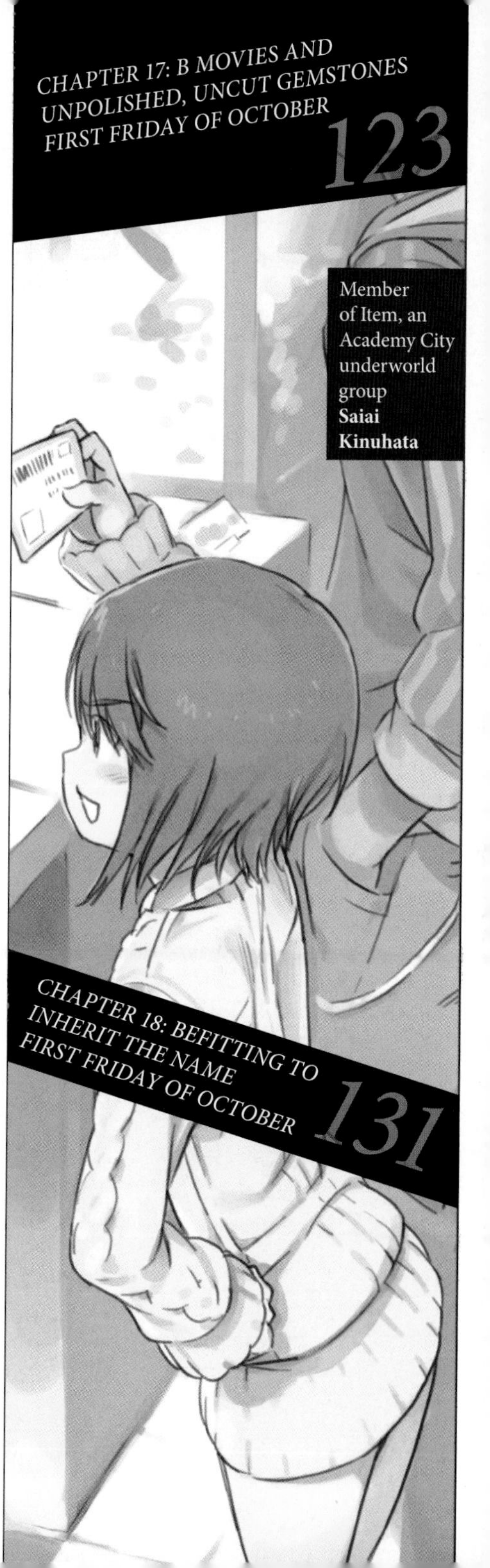
Member of Item, an Academy City underworld group **Saiai Kinuhata**

Mysterious
girl living in
Academy City
Seria Kumokawa

A Certain Magical Index SS

VOLUME 2

KAZUMA KAMACHI

ILLUSTRATION BY: KIYOTAKA HAIMURA

YEN ON

NEW YORK

A CERTAIN MAGICAL INDEX SS, Volume 2
KAZUMA KAMACHI

Translation by Andrew Prowse
Cover art by Kiyotaka Haimura

TOARU MAJYUTSU NO INDEX SS Vol.2
©Kazuma Kamachi 2008
Edited by Dengeki Bunko
First published in Japan in 2008 by KADOKAWA CORPORATION, Tokyo.
English translation rights arranged with KADOKAWA CORPORATION, Tokyo,
through Tuttle-Mori Agency, Inc., Tokyo.

English translation © 2021 by Yen Press, LLC

Yen On
150 West 30th Street, 19th Floor
New York, NY 10001

Visit us at yenpress.com
facebook.com/yenpress
twitter.com/yenpress
yenpress.tumblr.com
instagram.com/yenpress

First Yen On Edition: February 2021

Yen On is an imprint of Yen Press, LLC.
The Yen On name and logo are trademarks of Yen Press, LLC.

Library of Congress Cataloging-in-Publication Data
Names: Kamachi, Kazuma, author. | Haimura, Kiyotaka, 1973– illustrator. |
Prowse, Andrew (Andrew R.), translator.
Title: A certain magical index SS / Kazuma Kamachi ; illustration by
Kiyotaka Haimura ; translation by Andrew Prowse.
Other titles: Toaru majutsu no indekkusu SS. English
Description: First Yen On edition. | New York, NY : Yen On, 2020–
Identifiers: LCCN 2020041297 | ISBN 9781975317973 (v. 1 ; trade paperback) |
ISBN 9781975317997 (v. 2 ; trade paperback)
Subjects: CYAC: Magic—Fiction. | Ability—Fiction. | Schools—Fiction. |
Science fiction.
Classification: LCC PZ7.1.K215 Cer 2020 | DDC [Fic]—dc23
LC record available at https://lccn.loc.gov/2020041297

ISBNs: 978-1-9753-1799-7 (paperback)
978-1-9753-1800-0 (ebook)

1 3 5 7 9 10 8 6 4 2

LSC-C

Printed in the United States of America

CHAPTER 1

Those Seeking Riches and Battles

Third Friday of January

The station wagon sped through Academy City, an urban center built upon cleared land in the western part of Tokyo. In the vehicle were three young men: Ritoku Komaba, Shiage Hamazura, and a man known only as Hanzou. They belonged to a delinquent group named Skill-Out.

Hamazura, who was gripping the steering wheel, clearly wasn't old enough to have his driver's license yet. That couldn't be compared to the two other rules they were breaking, though.

The first was that the station wagon itself was a stolen vehicle.

The second was that an ATM, which they'd picked up using heavy machinery, was shoved in the backseat.

Their station wagon barreled along roads lined with wind turbines, driving along underneath blimps that drifted in the blue skies.

"Hoo, boy. You're telling me this one machine has, like, twenty million in it?" breathed Hanzou, his eyes glittering as he looked at the ATM, its screen shattered and chassis broken. Then, to Hamazura, the one right in front of him in the driver's seat at the wheel, he said, "I knew scouting you was a good idea. Without a guy who could tear out the machine's anti-earthquake reinforcements with construction equipment, there's no way we could've pulled this shit off."

"Wait, then how've you been getting money before now?"

"Hmm? Oh, I've just been stealing sheet metal and scampering away as fast as my little legs can carry me."

"That's so lame, though!!"

"To be honest, it would be way faster to drag some weakling into an alley and hit 'em a few times. But hey, Komaba's the type who doesn't lay a hand on weak little women and children."

"Well, now that we have this, we'll be livin' large for a while!!"

Hamazura and Hanzou bellowed laughter like a couple of idiots, but Komaba didn't react despite being mentioned. Hamazura checked the rearview mirror. The large, broad man just sat there silently like he was waiting on the sidelines for a chance that would never come.

"What's up with Komaba?"

"Ah. You probably noticed earlier. Back when some random guy tried running up on an elementary school with a crossbow—right at the beginning of the third term, too—Komaba punched him like five meters away with only his fist. After that surprising show of kindness, it's no wonder the little girl adores him. I'd think he's probably still really embarrassed."

Komaba, a hulking gorilla who could bring children to tears with just one look, gave a start, shifting his shoulders.

"Huh…? But I think he's on his PDA looking at an Internet shopping website. Staring at this XL-sized Santa outfit and white beard. Been all stiff for about ten minutes now."

Komaba twitched again—or wait, was he *trembling*?

"Well, you said it yourself, didn't you, leader? She was all, *Santa Claus really exists, right…?* And then he went, *Yeah, he'll come at the end of the year—a real roughneck Santa Claus!!*"

The pair of idiots continued their uproarious laughter, commenting on how there was no way that would ever happen when Komaba abruptly squeezed the PDA in his hand like it was a wet rag and shouted, "Graaaaaahhhhhhhhhh!!"

"Oh no! Did Komaba go insane from all the embarrassment?!"

And despite Komaba not exactly being seated at the steering wheel, the station wagon slid unnaturally to one side anyway.

*　　*　　*

"So, Hamazura, you're telling me there's a way to break into an ATM?" Hanzou asked as they continued on their way to the hideout.

"Uh, yeah. I'll handle the disassembly, too. There's a…what's it called? A capsule thing inside the safe. You can't be rough prying it open."

"A capsule?"

"Yeah, with fluorescent paint in it. If you don't open it properly, it'll mark all the bills, and then they're useless," explained Hamazura, adding in warning, "So don't touch it until we get to the hideout."

"Hamazura…what could this be, you think?"

"Damn it, Komaba!! I just told you not to touch it like five seconds ago—wait, what?"

Hamazura glanced at the rearview mirror, then stopped.

Between Ritoku Komaba's large fingers was a long, thin stick that looked like a USB drive.

Oh, shit. Hamazura paled.

In a subdued voice, Komaba muttered, "…It looks like a GPS transmitter, but…"

That was the exact moment a shrill siren started blaring right behind them. No one needed to check to know that the lights flashing behind them were red. It was a high-speed vehicle, based on a sports car—the sort of cruiser driven by Anti-Skill, the city's peacekeepers.

And right in front of them, in the middle of the road about a hundred meters up ahead, was a formation of specialized barricade robots: Giant and cylindrical, these machines were equipped with thick cushioning material all around. They looked like giant scrolls stood up on their sides as they rotated, unfurling to set up a soft, thick wall blocking off the road in the blink of an eye.

As the finishing touch, a few Anti-Skill cruisers slid to a stop right on the other side of the barricade, bolstering the rampart's defenses even further.

Hanzou's hands went to his head. "We're caught between a rock and a soft place! What the hell do we do now, Hamazura?!"

"What do we do?" repeated Hamazura, thinking for a moment. "Guess we break through."

The Anti-Skill officers waiting near the barricade dove aside as the suspects' car accelerated, its driver clearly flooring it. One officer rolled out of the passenger seat of her high-speed cruiser, which she'd parked on the road just in case—and a moment later, the station wagon smashed through, sending everything flying.

Eighty percent of Academy City's population was students, and as a result, the crimes that happened in Anti-Skill's jurisdiction were mostly juvenile offenses. Naturally, those responsible for maintaining the peace had developed and responded with that in mind.

The barricade robots' cushioning was for safely capturing children. It was too soft to spell instant death upon crashing, unlike a concrete block. In addition, since the parked cruisers were hit side-on, the station wagon had managed to pry open a gap between them, plunging through the barricade all at once while flinging metallic bumper parts all over.

The driver of the chase vehicle that had been pursuing the station wagon panicked, slamming on the brakes just moments before colliding with what was left of the barricade.

In the meantime, the station wagon took a sharp turn and disappeared past an intersection.

"Wow—just, wow!" laughed the officer as she watched them go from her vantage point on the pavement. They had certainly given her an eyeful. "I have the feeling I've found another interesting idiot—first time in a while, yeah?"

Hanzou craned his neck to check behind them, then whistled as he watched the scenery blurring away.

"That was crazy!!" he exclaimed. "I didn't know you could bust through that kind of barricade by force!"

"Well, it's important to figure out what kind of wall it is first,"

Hamazura cautioned. "If it was the kind that would have stopped the car even if it meant crushing us flat, or the kind that lets you go past so it can blow your tires out, doing what I did would've turned out way worse."

Meanwhile, Komaba—with a dispassionate look on his face—opened the car window and flung the GPS transmitter outside. "I guess we should probably switch to a different car now."

"Once we get a little farther. Doesn't look like anyone's behind us, but just in case—," Hamazura began before suddenly being cut off.

With a *vroom*, a large, specialized vehicle burst out from a side road. While its appearance resembled a tanker, its body was awfully angular and had a bunch of what seemed like armor stuck to it. In any case, it was an *extremely* rugged-looking truck.

"Gah?!"

Before Hamazura could react, the front of the enormous vehicle rammed into the back corner of the station wagon. The car's speed remained constant, but its heading was abruptly pushed sixty degrees to the side. The guardrail, which had been right next to them, was closely visible now. Instead of forcing the steering wheel back into its former position, Hamazura let the station wagon continue its slide to prevent it from spinning out completely.

The tires screeched, leaving streaks of black on the road. If he thoughtlessly hit the brakes, he'd instantly lose control. Instead, he expertly used the accelerator to regain stability.

"Shit! What was that?!" cried Hamazura as he looked behind him. And then his pupils shrank to dots.

The rig had little red lights sitting on its roof.

"Is this a joke?!" he shouted. "That thing can't possibly be one of Anti-Skill's cruisers, right?!"

At the same moment, the truck pursuing them made a sharp turn, swinging its rear tank around. It closed in like it had locked on to their station wagon.

Hanzou paled. "Oh, shit!! Looks like they're tryin' to kill us after all!!"

Meanwhile, the big-breasted woman in the driver's seat of the truck—looking like she'd probably flashed her badge and forcibly borrowed the vehicle—called something to them through a loudspeaker in one hand.

"Testing, testing. This is Aiho Yomikawa, Anti-Skill Branch Seven-Three. Robbery, property damage, interference of public duties, the list goes on—you assholes are going straight to hell, you hear me?"

"Damn it!! Listing interference of public duties last totally means that cow is pretty much after us over a grudge!" shouted Hanzou, taking out a handgun.

As if on cue, the truck sped closer with incredible horsepower.

Aiho Yomikawa sat in the driver's seat of the tanker, gripping the steering wheel—which was as big as a Hula-Hoop—and tried to overtake the station wagon. The man wearing a bandanna and holding a gun was getting ready to lean out of his window, but Yomikawa spun the steering wheel to the side before he could, whipping the tanker's tail end around and ramming it into the car.

A funny-sounding *karaaash* went off.

The station wagon was forced to keep driving straight, pinned between the large vehicle and the guardrail as it was; but the guardrail was what gave out first. The station wagon tore through its metal plating, and—having lost control—both it and the truck plowed right into an unmanned warehouse on the side of the road.

They destroyed the thick steel door, sending the piles of cardboard boxes inside the warehouse tumbling all over. Finally, the station wagon and the truck branched off, with the station wagon heading toward another cardboard mountain range and the truck crashing into one of the warehouse's inside walls.

Bsshhh!! The steering wheel airbag deployed, inflating directly into Yomikawa's face.

"*Urfh!* ...Those rotten little brats! I'll chase them to the ends of the earth in this thing!"

For now, she had to back out of the wall. She pulled on the gear-shift and stepped on the accelerator, but the truck wouldn't even budge.

By the time she realized the vehicle's crushed body had gotten tangled on something, she saw a few young men come out from the back of the warehouse, all holding guns.

"Not good," murmured Yomikawa, opening the driver's side door and rolling out.

An instant later, she heard a rapid *bang-bang-bang* of several bullets impacting the passenger side.

...A three-round burst? thought Yomikawa with a frown, taking cover behind the vehicle's tanker. Burst-fire was a mechanism that fired three bullets automatically with one pull of the trigger. The idea was to increase the rate of power while conserving ammunition, but...

"Ow!! Hanzou, are you stupid or something?! Why the hell'd you give this huge magnum a burst mode?! And you can't even switch to semi-auto!"

"What do you mean? Isn't it stronger and cooler when you can shoot a lot of bullets?"

"...Was that why you went to the trouble of extending the magazine?"

Great, they're all idiots, thought Yomikawa. *I should be able to manage this.*

A handgun modified like that would have so much recoil they'd never be able to hit anything they're aiming at. Yomikawa was assured of her victory, but suddenly, she noticed something rolling over to her from the rig. An object that looked to be about the size of a soccer ball.

"Ack!"

This time, she ran away as fast as she could.

The concept of Hanzou's custom burst-fire magnum was obviously idiotic, but it did pack an undeniable punch. Realizing it would be a good idea to keep the Anti-Skill officer from using the rig as cover, Hamazura focused his fire on the fuel tank near the bottom of the driver's seat.

When he did, he saw the officer frantically running away. She was probably worried the fuel tank would explode.

"Great, we drove her off. That stupid cow—actually, I wish we'd kidnapped her and made her pay for this."

"...I will not tolerate any sexual assault."

"Yeah, yeah. I know, Komaba. Anyway, the ATM. We don't want to get surrounded when she calls in reinforcements. Wonder if the car still moves..."

Then, as Hamazura started toward the station wagon, still stuck underneath a pile of cardboard boxes, something ran into his toes.

He looked down and saw a sphere about the size of a soccer ball on the floor.

A look of horror dawned on his face as Hanzou went white and Komaba—as usual—showed no emotion.

"Hey, Hamazura, isn't that...?"

"...Yeah..."

It was a huge firework—the kind you'd only see at organized events.

Another glance at the side of the tanker revealed letters reading Fukuoka Explosives. He also saw similar ball-shaped silhouettes scattered throughout the warehouse.

A moment later, there was a click and a flash.

The source was something that looked an awful lot like a torn electric cord, over by the fuel tank that had been underneath the driver's seat until it was blown off by the overpowered magnum. The tip of it shone with a light blue glow right before it plopped onto the gasoline spreading over the floor.

""""AH?!"""""

And thus, the three idiots' screams were drowned out by bright flowers blooming in the winter sky.

In the end, Hamazura, Hanzou, and Komaba—blown into the sky like the explosive end of a comedy sketch—were arrested by Yomikawa upon her return and thrown into a jail cell. Several other ill-bred-looking delinquent boys shared the room with them, but none of them so much as tried to meet eyes with Hamazura and the others, sensing something from how beat-up and covered in soot they were.

Hamazura, gripping the steel grating in both hands, bowed his head limply. "…I mean, sure, we did something bad by stealing an ATM. But wasn't that cow even worse?! And all the bills inside the ATM ended up getting burned anyway!!"

"…A fearsome Anti-Skill officer, indeed, when it would actually have been less destructive for her to simply let criminals go free and not pursue them… So they truly exist: Those outrageously happy-go-lucky types you see in detective shows… It seems we cannot underestimate that busty woman…"

"Gah, damn it!! Komaba, she doesn't count as a kid or some weak little girl, right?! We gotta break out of here somehow and make her pay, with some squeezing and smooshing, like this…!!"

Hamazura wasn't the only one complaining—even the usually taciturn Komaba was muttering. But it seemed like Hanzou hadn't been listening for some time now. The explosive fireworks display must have been quite a shock for him, because he'd been sitting in the corner of the cell, arms wrapped around his knees, completely still.

Eventually, appearing to have come to a decision, he opened his mouth slowly.

"Sorry. Hamazura—and Komaba—I'm sorry. I really am."

"Eh? What's going on?"

The two of them looked over, and Hanzou looked away, as if unable to endure their gazes.

What he said was short and simple.

"…I think I'm in love."

""Urgh?!""

CHAPTER 2

The Warrior and the Dancer from Norse Mythology
First Friday of February

In one small jeans shop in London:

"No more of this, girlfriend. I'm not selling you anything."

"Wh-why not?!" cried Kaori Kanzaki, slamming her hands on the counter with a *bam*. "I always bring payment along with me! Even when you're charging me an arm and a leg for vintage ones with ambiguous market value, even though I include a tip for you—and why won't you look at me?!"

"Well, just *look* at you, honey!!" The owner pointed sharply at Kanzaki's thigh area.

The jeans she was wearing had one leg completely cut off at the thigh, granting her an asymmetrical sort of beauty as well as an unadorned sexiness.

"I work *so* hard, going all over the world for these vintage jeans, only to have you cut them up!! You don't seem to understand how much that pair is worth—it was made with all sorts of special features meant for the men working the mines during the California gold rush…!!"

"I understand that. That's why I'm always sure to make the part I cut off into a purse, like this one—"

"Aaaaaaaaaaaaaaaaaaaagh!!" roared the owner like a raging bull, running his hands through his hair. "Anyway, I'm not selling anything to you, and I'm not going to help you with your work, either! If you don't like it, then go cry to the god of jeans and premium goods and apologize to them!!"

"I…I see. I haven't even explained the details yet… But you say you will not aid me in my work. That is a shame…" Kanzaki's shoulders drooped. "That just means I'll have to deal with them alone—the mysterious jeans-snipping slasher being whispered about on the streets."

"You should've said that sooner!"

Kaori Kanzaki's job was to take down evil sorcerers.

It wasn't the most specific job, and it seemed like an occupation best left for storybooks—but they existed, and that was that. And since the organization she belonged to was connected to their state religion, she quietly earned a stable income that was about what a civil servant could expect to make. This was how the hard-earned money of UK taxpayers paid for nebulous activities and expenses.

Like out of a storybook… Kanzaki laughed at herself a little. Right now, thanks to certain circumstances, her heart was sealed shut on a deep level—although humans are creatures who cannot hold a single emotion in their heart for very long. Without twisting a person's fundamental personality to an irreparable level, their innate senses of duty and compassion will eventually surface when they least expect it.

"Come to think of it, what *did* happen to that Stiyl?" asked the owner.

Stiyl was a colleague of Kanzaki's. "He's following the child," she answered.

"He's *still* going on about that?"

"……"

"Well, not that I have any right to criticize him. We just have to pray some idiot doesn't dash in like a hero," said the owner before pausing and changing the topic. "Actually, Kanzaki, aren't you cold in that getup? It's February, and it's freezing."

The owner was hugging himself, shivering fiercely. Februaries in

London fell squarely in the wintertime. And this year, a severe cold wave had hit the entire nation—the kind where the story about the match-selling girl who died made perfect sense. It was cold enough that some ponds had frozen solid, and now anyone could walk across them.

But even though Kanzaki's thigh was completely exposed—albeit just the one—she replied, "No, not especially."

"Unbelievable…," the shop owner muttered, his lips turning blue and his breath white, while wearing heavy gear that he could have scaled Mount Everest in. "Anyway, what's this about a jeans-snipping slasher?"

"It's just what it sounds like. A mystery person, identity unknown, who cuts only the jeans of those they pass by. The only notable damages thus far have been jeans—no one has been injured, apparently."

"We can kill them, right?"

"You decided on that faster than the speed of sound."

"Now that I think about it…the jeans-snipping slasher, eh…? Surprised *you* weren't suspected."

"??? Why would anyone suspect me of this?"

The owner gave a sigh at the confused, thigh-exhibitionist girl standing before him. "Never mind. Any clues where they're hiding?"

"Yes, but not much of one. The criminal's actions have the smell of Norse mythology."

"…Any proof of that? Who investigated this?"

"Theodosia."

"Her? I suppose we should take that with a grain of salt— Oh."

As the owner and Kanzaki watched, they saw an old bearded man suddenly stumble, lose all his energy, and collapse. The jeans he was wearing had been severed cleanly at both thighs; the tragic transformation made them look more like briefs than jeans.

The owner unwittingly covered his face with his hands. "Damn, that's awful… They just robbed a proud English gentleman of all his dignity. They didn't even leave him with the energy to fix his own beard!!"

"Indeed. If they were going to cut them, they could have done it with a little more class, like I do."

"I am definitely not selling you anything ever again."

Just then, Kanzaki heard a sharp noise like metal plates scraping together.

Almost like scissors.

"?!"

It almost got her.

Kanzaki whipped around, swinging the long, sheathed katana she carried at nearly the same moment an unknown attacker closed in on her with a blade. Two silhouettes crossed. A silly *ba-bam* went off, but for the moment, Kanzaki's jeans hadn't turned into denim briefs.

"Who are you?!" Kanzaki shouted, glaring harshly at her opponent.

The rumored surprise-tailor turned out to be a woman about the same age as Kanzaki. She was slender and well proportioned, with hair that was closer to silver than blond. Her clothing consisted of several pieces of steel positioned in a particular way to form a unique set of breastplate and waist armor; her hands were in long gloves that reached above the elbow; and her legs sported long boots above tights that were, for some reason, white and black in a cow pattern, and wait a minute.

Kanzaki's eyes shrank to pinpoints.

The shop owner's eyes goggled. Trembling, he said:

"That's gotta be...the legendary *bikini armor*."

Flustered at the incredible sight before her eyes, Kanzaki said, "Umm, well, where do I even start with this...?!! I mean, the top part—there's barely anything there. So how about I start with that?!"

The mysterious exhibitionist stuck out her ridiculously ample chest. "Your own shirt is quite the same, I'd say. Even I find myself in awe and admiration of its sexiness."

"...!!"

"Hang on a sec there, Kanzaki!! It's too soon to draw your blade!! And if you ask me, you *are* way too erotic, from an objective point of view!!"

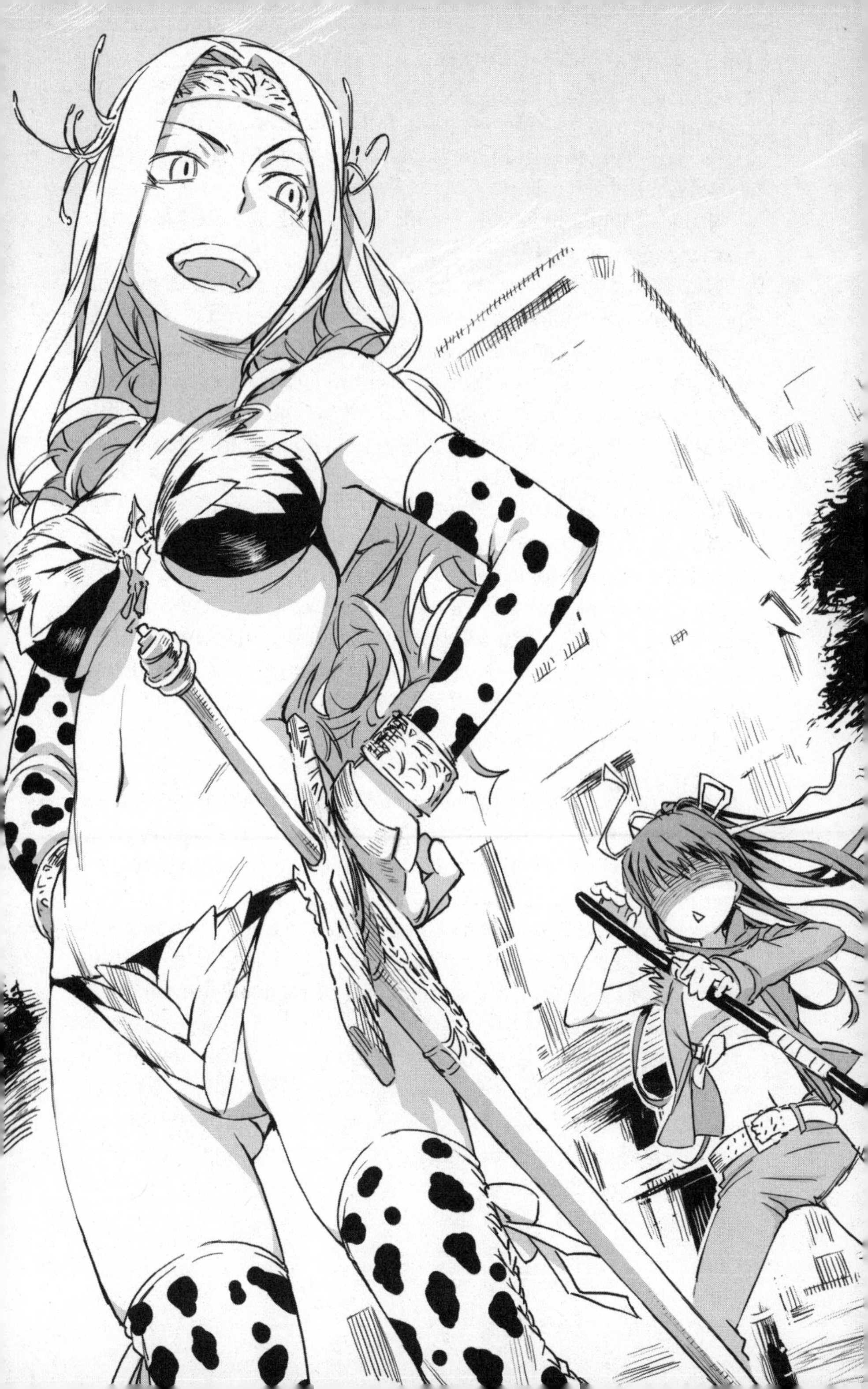

"Why are you putting me in a full nelson and agreeing with her?! Have you forgotten we're about to *fight* that exhibitionist jean-slasher?!"

"No, we might still be able to talk things out!! We need to do the best we can, right now!!"

"Is… Is that so? To tell the truth, I've already started to give up about halfway!! Could you please deal with that pervert?!"

"We just have to hold on a little longer!! From a clothing specialist's point of view, it's true that her outfit is out of fashion. Cow-skin patterns don't hold any special meaning anymore! Why, all she's doing is showing off those boobs of hers!! After all, this whole time my eyes have been glued to—"

"You're just completely falling for her trap, aren't you?!"

Kanzaki let loose a punch to catapult the owner meters away from her, like a kung fu movie.

The bikini-clad woman in question laughed softly at the display. It was a quiet, alluring tittering that was at odds with her outfit. "I cannot blame the gentleman for his excitement. That is, after all, the meaning behind the Valkyries' existence."

Valkyries?

In Norse mythology, they were humans referred to as heavenly maidens, or battle maidens. It was said their duty was to deliver the souls of warriors to Valhalla, in preparation for Ragnarok. But some postulated they were actually angels or spirits—something that had never been human. A maiden born as a human could apparently become a Valkyrie by desiring battle over all else and satisfying certain conditions to be granted power by the chief god Odin. In other words, it was a path that dauntless and courageous women could walk to be apotheosized.

If humans could indeed become Valkyries, it wasn't unusual to think that a group residing in the world of sorcery might just try to do so artificially. Sorcery was like a lab-grown diamond. The system was completely dedicated to bringing about normally rare, miraculous events on demand. Wanting to create a simple homemade recipe for becoming a Valkyrie—well, the idea wasn't *wrong*, exactly.

"…And why exactly is a Valkyrie apprentice doing this…? The last I checked, there weren't any spirits of macho men in this neck of the woods."

The Valkyrie tsked. "Transporting the souls of warriors is not the only duty of the Valkyries. More important is that we pour wine for the gentlemen invited to Valhalla, perform our dances for them, and bind and 'educate' their minds for the sake of Valhalla. My goal is to use my charms to create more Einherjar, thus single-handedly accumulating power rivaling that of an entire sorcerer society.

"In conclusion!!" continued the battle maiden, sticking out her chest even further. "At times to fight, at times to dance, always girding oneself with heroism and beauty—the logical conclusion of *this* Valkyrie, I must say, resides within the very way I present myself!! Indeed, as a dancing girl in sexy armor!!"

…So not only her armor was off the rails but her mind was, too?

For a moment, and just a moment, Kanzaki had uncharacteristically given up on everything about this. But she shook her head and managed to reject it. Kanzaki's magic name was Salvere000: the hand of salvation for the unsaved. She couldn't allow herself to give up now.

But she couldn't deny that this was a ridiculous situation. "All right!" she shouted. "I'm fully disappointed now, so let's make sure we talk things over as we fight!!"

"Ha-ha!! I am she who hath abandoned her humanity, even donning such embarrassing clothing as this! A mere sorceress off the streets hath not the strength to stop me!!"

"So you *do* feel embarrassed about it! That means there's hope for you yet…!!"

Kanzaki was getting fairly worked up herself, but the sexy Valkyrie's attack had enough speed, weight, and power to be worthy of the title Valkyrie. And she rammed her blade into Kanzaki's over and over again, too.

"Behold, the true power of a Valkyrie—it's a Party of Nine!!"

After chanting something or other loudly, the Valkyrie's shadow suddenly split into nine at her feet. The strange shadows almost seemed to be forming a magic circle, and this set Kanzaki on her guard.

"?!"

The nine shadows didn't really do anything, though. They whirled around the Valkyrie for a bit, then just disappeared. Kanzaki was confused, until—

"Mhhoooooohhhhhhhhhhhhhhhhhh?!"

—a scream suddenly rose from the jeans shop owner's throat, shaking the very air.

What, what? What happened? Kanzaki looked his way. The owner, who had collapsed, rose back onto his feet, his movements awkward and stunted. No, wait—nine maidens? She wasn't sure where they came from, but they grabbed him by the hands, legs, waist, and neck and were moving him around by force.

"Hoh-hoh-hoh," chuckled the Valkyrie. "When magically supporting a warrior, a Valkyrie does it with a group of nine. My spell uses nine maidens to control a gentleman and make him my pawn!!"

"What about his mind?"

"Frankly, the more they see my body and think 'this is the most incomparable expression of feminine beauty that I've ever seen! You are truly too beautiful for this world!! I want to abandon all my friends, my women, and my life, sell them away, and serve you and you alone!! Actually, with that kind of beauty, how are you not a god yet?'—the easier it is to trap them in my spell, if you must know."

Which means, the moment someone becomes too aroused by her sexy bikini outfit, they fall under her control, thought Kanzaki, reviewing the situation as she regarded the shop owner with cold eyes.

He looked away from Kanzaki somewhat awkwardly and mumbled a "sorry."

Kanzaki simply nodded. "Off with your head, then."

"Wait, wait, Kanzaki!! My sense of justice is all helter-skelter in my brain right now!! I'll break free of this cowardly sorcery with love and justice—just you wait, I will show you what a man is truly made of!!"

Just then, the Valkyrie bent over in his direction. She placed her palms on her knees, squeezed her breasts between her arms, and gave a quick wink. "Kill her, and I'll show you all *kinds* of things. Would you like to be top or bottom?"

"…Sorry, Kanzaki. My heart—it's changing so fast right now that I don't think I can reel it back—"

"Off with your head, then."

Apparently, Kanzaki was still willing to offer a modicum of mercy since she hit him with the dull edge of her blade, sending the sulky shopkeeper flying into the skies above London.

Having purged the traitor, Kanzaki prepared to restart the battle, but first, she cut to the heart of this curious incident. "By the way, why are you only cutting the jeans of gentlemen?"

"Ah, yes. My field of specialty when it comes to entertaining warriors is erotic humiliation."

I'll have to beat her down 20 percent harder. She was being a public nuisance, after all.

CHAPTER 3

A Father's Wish Is for Contact and Exchange

Fourth Friday of February

After Valentine's Day, February was as good as garbage.

So thought the middle-aged father, Touya Kamijou, but then…

"Oh, right. There was a carnival here in Europe, wasn't there?"

When Touya thought of *carnavals*, he thought of those big events in Brazil, where the young ladies wearing peacock-like accessories swung their hips from side to side really fast, but apparently they didn't have any of those peacock girls here in Italy. That was too bad. Here, with men and women going about with masks that looked like they were made of glass, the view was more surreal—actually, if they went into a department store like that, someone would probably call the police.

Anyone who got that glimpse into his thoughts would realize that Touya Kamijou was not affiliated with any particular religion, nor did he differentiate between global religions, new age religions, and cults. No, he was a typical Japanese man, one who would simply wonder what festival this was again.

So he decided to ask the part-time girl working at the local souvenir shop, located in a tent on the corner of the cobblestone road.

"Oh, yes, sir. Lent is going to start soon. This festival is for stuffing ourselves with food before the coming fast, but, uhhh, a lot of stuff has gotten mixed in with the tradition over the years. Kind of like how the sambas for Rio's *carnaval* originally came from religious African music, then grew into its own thing."

"Another ambiguous one… Are those masks official, then?"

"Doubt it. People just bring them here because they think Venetian customs are cool. Glass masks aren't part of the traditional crafts here in Milan. Hey, you want to buy one?"

The blond-haired, blue-eyed part-timer smiled, recommending a souvenir that wasn't even local.

Touya, half appalled, said, "Ha-ha. You don't understand the basics of business."

"Huh? The Carnival only happens once a year—you're not a tourist who came for it?"

"I actually just clocked out, believe it or not. Finished up a bit of a business talk."

Touya was a sales representative for a foreign-owned enterprise.

…Which may make it sound like he was just an average salaryman, but his actual occupation was fairly irregular. Strictly speaking, he belonged to a department called the Office of Securities Trading Prevention.

His job was to use any means at his disposal to stop stock trading, mergers, and the like that would be harmful to his own company. The post was beginning to be seen as even more important now that anyone could use a computer to buy and sell stocks in a matter of a few hours.

This sort of securities trading was, as a rule, something that could be done relatively freely, and since the global market straddled national borders, it was difficult for a single country to legally control…but that was a different issue. The mere eleven people belonging to the Office of Securities Trading Prevention were the best of the best—they'd put all their knowledge and technique to use from fields like economics and psychology and freely bent the rules in gray areas in order to do their jobs.

Well, broadly speaking, it's okay to tell them, "You might take a huge loss if you buy up all these securities" but not "Hey, don't buy those securities."

"What would I know about business, anyway? As you can see, I'm a regular part-timer. There's no business plan here. I'm standing out on the side of the road, just like the little match girl."

"Let's start there. You should have more confidence in the products you're selling. The reason *ennichi* yakisoba looks so appetizing isn't because of the festival atmosphere around it. It's because of the way the old guy at the stall cooks it."

"What's *en-nee-chee* mean?"

"It's the same reason they codified customer service in chain restaurants. Seeing employees with inconsistent levels of confidence is enough to affect how patrons look at the place. That's why restaurants promote a standardized, average level of confidence that all employees should be able to project."

"Anyway, are you going to buy one or not? I mean, I really don't mind if you're just window-shopping, 'cause it passes the time."

Touya sighed. She truly didn't have any enthusiasm. "I'm looking for an Italian souvenir. Something you can look at and immediately know I went to Italy. Something everyone would be delighted to see. Bonus points for having some kind of casual boon from a god or something."

"Oh, right, I see. You're looking for local good-luck charms. Japanese people really like ambiguous things like that, huh?" replied the part-timer offhandedly, fishing around in a nearby pile of items. "How about this? Dollar bills sure to summon good fortune. I'll let you have them for one hundred euros if you buy now."

"Italy doesn't even use dollars to begin with."

"I'll get a receipt for you. Otherwise it'll be considered tax evasion, here in Italy."

"Wait. I haven't even bought anything, so don't print a receipt for it. You're being a very pushy saleswoman."

"...That's strange. I heard Japanese people will buy just about anything if you tell them it brings good luck," she muttered.

Then, as if spotting something, her face paled. Frantically, she got all the items in order, then pulled a single string to fold up the tent, completing her preparations to flee in just fifteen seconds.

As Touya watched, flabbergasted at how fast she was, the part-timer said, "Crap, the weirdo is here! Sorry, sir! If we're lucky, maybe we'll meet again!!"

"Huh? Ummm, what?"

"Someone who doesn't tolerate selling such ambiguous souvenirs is approaching fast!! She's especially strict about ripping off Japanese sightseers in particular! As a parting gift, I'll tell you the three things I hate most: my parents, my teacher, and missionaries!!" she rattled off, shouldering the piles of goods, the rolled-up tent joined to her backpack like a mountain climber's sleeping bag, and quickly rushing off.

"If we're lucky," huh? She certainly seems like she believes in luck, at least..., thought Touya, left behind with his peculiar impression. He stood dazed for a few moments.

"...Mgh. I'm certain that mana specific to Balbina was emitted somewhere in this area..."

All of a sudden, someone appeared, muttering suspicious-sounding Italian under her breath. It was a woman, dressed in a mainly white nun's habit that looked old-fashioned and worn. She was in either her late twenties or early thirties. Clearly, she had once been a beauty, but everything about her seemed strangely faded, like she alone was living in a damaged roll of film.

The nun squatted down in the space where the part-timer had her shop set up just moments ago, then slowly held her palm to the ground.

"It's still warm, as I expected. Which would mean... That brat ran away on me again! You there, sir—have you spotted a dull-looking lamb going through her rebellious phase around here?"

Touya was taken aback at the sudden mention, but eventually, he said, "No. The only one I saw was a young woman with quite charming freckles."

"If I could, I would deduct all points for that nauseating sentence and smile. What were you doing here in the first place, sir?"

"I was looking for an Italian souvenir. What about you, by the way? Are you her guardian or her teacher?"

Touya asked that specifically because they'd been examples of what the girl said she hated.

"No."

But it seemed neither was the case. Which meant there was only one answer left.

"I am a Roman Orthodox missionary. My name is Lidvia Lorenzetti. If you have an interest in our lord and savior—or have any ideas as to where our Balbina went after she snuck out of the morning sermon to earn a little cash—please contact us."

...That was the story anyway, but Touya Kamijou managed to coincidentally run into the missionary Lidvia five times in that day alone.

"Why are you always standing in places Balbina would likely go?"

"I told you, I'm just looking for an Italian souvenir. She simply happens to be everywhere I'm going. Anyway, why *does* the little stall keeper run away so fast every time you show up?"

"Hm? If you're looking for souvenirs, they're sold everywhere. Look over there—Milan cookies and Milan sweet bread. All you need to do is buy something and go home already."

"...Wait, they sell sweet buns in Italy?"

"I believe Japan, too, has a pasta dish called Napolitan. I should think you have no need to acquire the extravagant 'products' that Balbina is likely to sell."

"Well, there's a bit of a story behind my shopping, actually," said Touya, giving a relatively exhausted sigh. "Do you believe in rotten luck?"

"Hm?"

"I do. Because I've seen it. To tell the truth, my only child—a boy—has terribly rotten luck. He doesn't do anything bad to deserve it, either, but he's always getting caught up in trouble. It's become such a normal thing that whenever something unfortunate happens to him, everyone around him can't do anything but point and laugh."

Touya spoke while poking a small doll in a different stall with a finger.

"…I'm pathetic, aren't I? I can complain all I want about the people around him, but in the end, I haven't been able to do anything for him, either. I think maybe it will help if I buy a lot of good-luck charms, but maybe even *that* is nothing but a way for me to comfort myself. It's just an excuse to let me say that I'm doing my best—more than everyone else is."

Lidvia said nothing. Touya figured he was just being a bother by suddenly confiding in her, but he found he couldn't stop himself.

"To tell the truth, I want to get rid of his burdens myself. I'm his father, you know? But what can I do against an invisible opponent like misfortune? I'm truly pathetic. And an idiot for clinging to things like this."

"Heh…"

Then, before he knew it, Lidvia was hanging her head. *What could be wrong?* wondered Touya.

"Heh-heh. That's wonderful—truly wonderful. That trouble of yours… Being thrust into a situation where you can do nothing at all about it… Everything… Everything about this is…"

"U-umm—eek?!"

Touya sucked in a breath. For some reason, Lidvia was smiling. And it wasn't the kind of smile that would set someone at ease. It was a wide smile meant for herself, the sort where if she wasn't careful, she'd start drooling all over the place.

"Wonderful!! What wonderful impossibility! What wonderful absurdity!! The more difficult the situation grows, the more dramatically one's enthusiasm waxes!! Hee-hee—you wish to remove the misfortune clinging to your son, yes? In that case, the matter is simple. Balbina! Balbina—the magic herbalist, Balbinaaaaaaaaaaaaaa!!"

Shouting, Lidvia burst into a small alley at Mach speed, then came back just ten seconds later dragging the part-timer by the back of her neck. The girl, Balbina, pouted angrily as she slid along the ground.

"Ow, ow, that hurts!! What the heck?! Can't I just have a part-time job?! Is that so much to ask?!"

"It isn't the time for that! We have a situation—blah-blah, this and that!!"

"Geh!! You moron! Why didn't you tell me this was about helping someone out?!"

The two Italians seemed to be extremely agitated about something or other—Touya couldn't quite keep up. Lidvia and Balbina continued to become more heated, ignoring the perplexed middle-aged man. Balbina removed several things from her bag to show to the clueless Touya, like a strange doll and something that looked like dead grass, then packed them all in on top of a small notepad.

"For now, I gathered everything you don't need incantations or ceremonies for—stuff that's effective just from leaving it be! As for their safekeeping, all you need to do is read the warnings here and here!!"

"We wouldn't want some anti-sorcerer organization to set eyes on him. What about covering it up?"

"No worries, no problem!! Each one of these is still considered a Soul Arm, but they're not specialized for specific people, so none of them are worth getting punished for. Your strange souvenir problem is solved. This is gray-area stuff, close to white, so even a pro sorcerer would have trouble telling the difference!!"

""Anyway, you'll be fine!!"" cried both of them at the same time, giving their seal of approval. And then, to top it all off, Lidvia took out a Bible and half forced it into Touya's pocket.

"If it still doesn't work, please go to the nearest church. We build those roofs specifically to protect lambs tormented by undeserved calamity!!"

"Ha… Ha-ha. I see," said Touya, chuckling a little. "To be honest, I can't bring myself to believe in God like that. But if kind people like you believe in him, then maybe I can, too."

In that same city, Oriana Thomson, a huge-breasted smuggler who always acted in tandem with Lidvia, had just alluringly stuck out her tongue to engage in close-quarters combat with some gelato when her partner suddenly appeared as she hurtled toward her at a break-neck pace before finally tackling her.

"Orianaaaaaaaaaaaaaaaaaaaaaaaaaaaaaaaa!!"

"Nghagh?!"

The blow bent Oriana's carefully honed body over at the gut and sent her ice cream flying as both plopped onto the ground. Without paying the slightest bit of attention to the trembling smuggler, Lidvia was rapidly wiggling her hips around for some reason, hands on her cheeks.

"Th-this day!! What a good day this day is!! I may have been prisoner to a misunderstanding when it comes to Japanese people! I had thought they were the enemies of our society because of that barbaric Academy City—but to think it was home to fathers who cared so much for their children!! It may be that we will need to change our plan of conquest to a warmer, more peaceful one!!"

"What…? What do you mean…? Why's she so excited…?" Oriana asked Balbina after a bit of trouble breathing—she'd probably been dragged here by Lidvia. Blah-blah and so on. After hearing the story, Oriana pretended to worry for a moment.

"I… I see. Well, I mean… Ugh. At it again with the upper—"

"Oooooookaaaaaaaaaaaaaaaaaaaaaaaayyyyyyyyyyyy!!" yelled Lidvia suddenly before she could finish. Her swiftly undulating hips banged right into Oriana, sending her sliding to the side. Hearing an awful *kee-rack*, Balbina paled.

Without a care, Lidvia said, "Let's keep up our enthusiasm! Troubles are troubling because they are not easily resolved! And for those who do not understand the fun inherent in them, we shall resolve all their troubles for them!! First, we must prepare the Soul Arm. As it's so heavily affected by the positions of stars, we will first need to conduct observations on-site in order to use it at the appropriate coordinates!!"

With Lidvia being excruciatingly gung ho, Balbina began, once again, to flee. Oriana attempted to do the same, but before she could, Lidvia captured the smuggler.

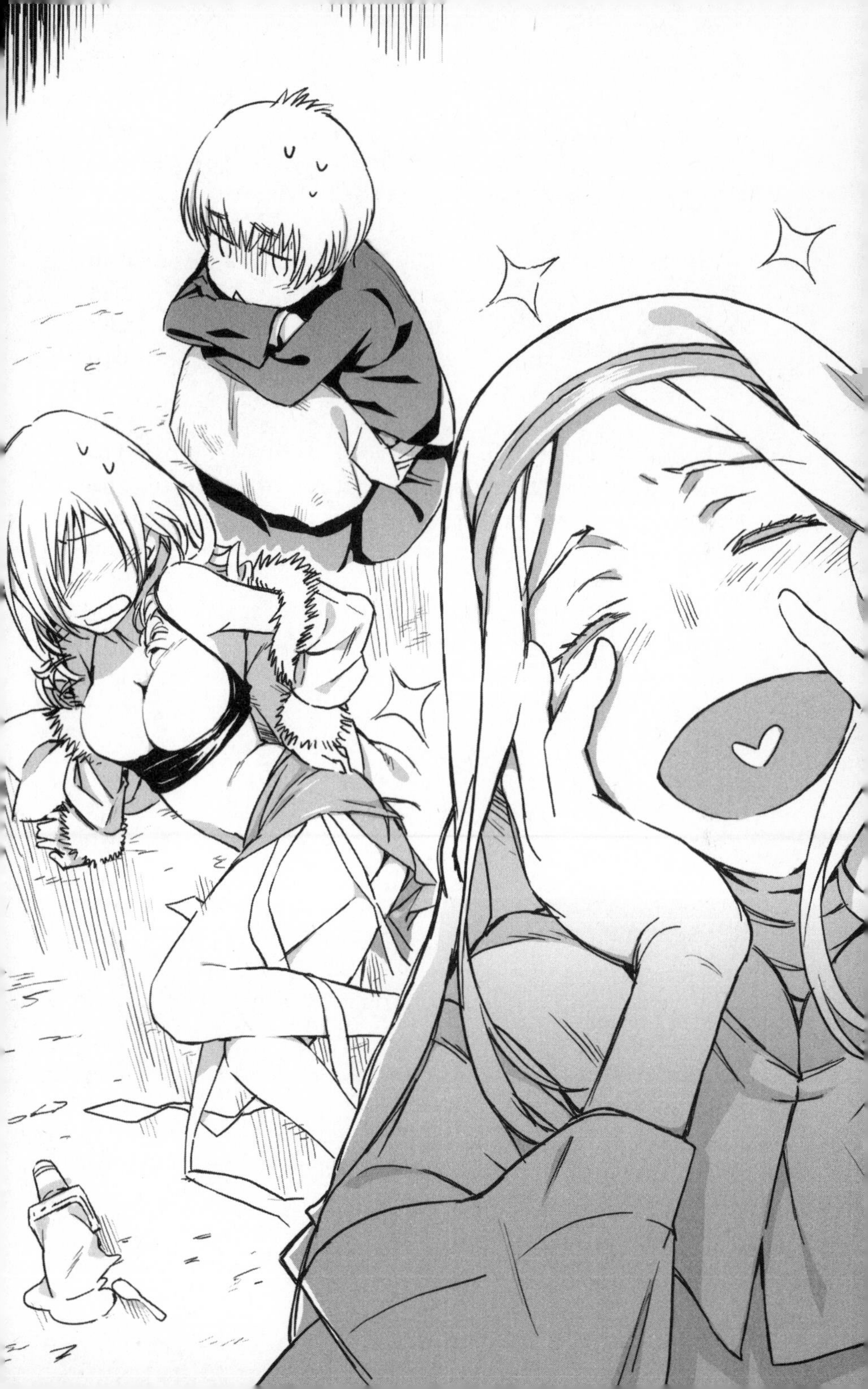

CHAPTER 4

The True Power of the Seventh Among Seven
Third Friday of March

8:10 PM, March 15.

White Day had been relatively uneventful, and now, the day after, Yabumi Haratani was nonchalantly wandering around the shopping district when some real bad dudes—Skill-Out—grabbed him by the collar and dragged him into a dank, pitch-black alley. This was exactly the kind of trouble a manga protagonist would get himself into. In any case, after being punched a few times and having his wallet confiscated, they took his cell phone as well, since it had a wallet function on it. He'd have to contact the service center quick or else he'd be the victim of a massive credit card theft catastrophe. However...

"Sweet. Stopping the phone seems like a fuckin' pain, so let's just tie him up around here and buy time, eh?"

"Oh? You sure? City birds are pretty violent. Leave defenseless meat lyin' around, and they'll snatch it right up."

"Digital wallets are so handy. No withdrawal limits, so long as we squeeze the number out of him."

Gyaaaaaaahhhhhhhhhhhhhhhhhh?! I shouldn't have taken the lady at the service center up on her recommendation to switch to a phone with new features I don't even use!!

Indeed, for if this had been a shakedown in the past, they would have just taken his wallet and let him go. Truly fearsome were these conveniences of civilization. User-side danger had evolved greatly just by carrying everyday items.

Surrounded by five or six slightly older boys, the cornered Haratani began to think, as any normal person would, about how he was going to bust out of this crisis.

"You don't have enough *guts*, dude. Nobody's gonna be satisfied with that!!"

A loud voice suddenly rang out.

He looked that way and saw a figure standing tall and firm at the alleyway's entrance.

For just a moment, the five or six young men were quiet, looking toward the figure.

Ba-bang!!

Before he could discern who the figure was, a delinquent boy abruptly took out a gun and fired it.

The mystery figure fell over with a *plop*. The delinquent tsked, seemingly irritated at the interruption. *What the hell was that awful plot twist?!* complained Haratani to himself and God.

"*Hoowwwraaaahhhhhhhhhhh!!*"

But then the shooting victim rose back up with a lunge. Seeing a person bouncing back up like a self-righting doll in just three seconds, even the young men were thrown off.

The stranger, who had clearly been shot in the heart, stomped closer with the strange enthusiasm of someone who had just pulled an all-nighter.

"Shooting me without any warning? You really *don't* have any guts. Or is it patience? Is it patience you lack? Given all this, the lot of you must be part of this new generation that gets pissed off too easily!! Haven't you ever regretted how the media takes huge dumps all over you whenever they can?!"

One of the delinquents, probably thinking, *He's not making sense, so let's shoot him again,* pulled the trigger a few more times. But by now, the mystery figure was only giving jolts—it wasn't even falling down.

The boy, obviously peeved by this, glanced down at the gun in his hands. "…Why won't you die…?"

"Because I have *guts!!*"

"That can't possibly be all it is!!"

"If you must know, I am Gunha Sogiita, one of Academy City's Level Fives and number seven of seven. But that barely matters— what we should be discussing right now is the sheer *guts* bubbling up, boiling within me, like a raging wave on stormy seas!!"

Sogiita—the inscrutable guts guy—howled the proclamation into the skies, his arms outstretched and his back bent over like a bow.

Haratani watched, completely baffled.

The delinquents huddled up a little and began to whisper things among themselves.

"If he's number seven out of seven, that means he's the weakest Level Five, right?"

"Then Level Zeroes like us should be able to manage."

One person couldn't stay silent at that, though—the number seven in question. "*Non, non!!* I told you all that Level Five stuff and number seven stuff was just a boring side trip!! What's important right now is the topic of my *guts!!* It's not too late, you know! Listen to what I have to say—*ow?!* Damn, don't hit me with a bicycle chain lock! Stop stabbing me with an ice pick! Ow, ow, ow! Stop it, you gutless fiends!!"

The scene was like some kind of joke, but if this was a two-hour-long suspense film, ten films' worth of footage could have been gleaned from this storm of violence.

And when Gunha Sogiita still wouldn't die, the belligerent delinquents were instead the ones feeling that things were eerie (though they didn't let up at all).

"*Daaahhhhhrrrraaaahhhsshaaaaaaaaaaaaaaaaaaaaaaaaaaaa!!*"

The instant the enraged Number Seven screamed, a strange explosion went off, centered on him. *Bwoom!!* It made a noise like a sound effect from a *tokusatsu* show, mowing down all the villains.

"How dare you do whatever you please!! I won't tolerate it any longer! I'll show you what *true* guts look like, so feast your eyes on this!!"

...Unfortunately for his one-sided burst of enthusiasm, every last one of the delinquents was already knocked out from the first hit. If he attacked a second time in this situation, it would doubtlessly make it much less clear who was the real villain. *And aren't the delinquents the ones who will end up showing their guts now anyway?* thought Haratani, somewhat more calmly.

And then it happened.

"Heh. Guess we couldn't get any more out of small-fries like them."

A newcomer appeared, beyond the darkness. The *shhh* of a footstep announced the approach of an urban nightmare born from the underworld of Academy City. One look at the enormous human weapon made Haratani want to ask him if this guy really had fought across at least three countries as part of a foreign mercenary team or if he just looked that way.

"I am Yokosuka the Organ Crusher. It looks like you took good care of these boys, eh?"

Lower-middle-class Yabumi wondered why, if this guy was really so great, he was stooping to back-alley shakedowns and not working on grand plans to topple foundational pillars of the world? Of course, the voice in his mind did not reach this final boss-looking man.

"But it looks like you've stuck your neck in where you shouldn't have. Regrets will do you no good here. Now that you stand before the great Yokosuka the Organ Crusher, an expert at anti-esper combat, you shall—"

"I'm really sorry, but I just farted!!"

"Ah— Hey! Shut up and listen to me until I'm done talking!! So—errr, right. Where was I again? Ah, yes. Ahem. Now that you stand before the great Yokosuka the Organ Crusher, you—"

"Awesome *puuunch*!"

"I *told* you to listen to what I'm—*blargh*?!"

Yokosuka the organ-playing whatever was cut off, suddenly spinning around like a bamboo helicopter. Haratani could swear that Number Seven and Organ Player were over ten meters apart; that weird impact, was it psychokinesis or something? Either way, it was a perfectly clean hit.

"I, *blurgh*. What…? What was that…?"

"Mm-hmm-hmm. That? Just the *true worth* of Academy City's number seven. I created an intentionally unstable psychokinetic wall in front of my body, then used my fist to deliver an impact that broke it, sending the explosive aftermath flying from a distance. If you've ever heard of my killer move, the Psycho Cannon, that was it!!"

Ba-baaam!! A new truth revealed to the public.

But Haratani calmly stated, "Nah, that's impossible."

"?"

"I doubt you'd get that kind of reaction if all you did was provide a pulse of energy to an unstable psychokinetic wall. I chose psychokinetics as my optional course in the Ability Development curriculum, so I know a thing or two about it."

"……"

"……"

The puncher and the punchee both fell into an awkward silence.

After clenching his fist and looking at the ground for a short time, Sogiita said, "Then what explains it, and what came out?"

"Hhhhheeeeeeeeeeeeyyyyyyyyyyy!! That's so random! What a sketchy killer move!! Why don't you try putting yourself in the shoes of the people you take down with that, damn it?!"

"Awesome *puuunch*!"

"It's literally the same as be—*florgh?!*"

Around and around he went, spinning away, the organ-playing Yokosuka.

For some reason, I'm not happy at all that I've been saved, thought Haratani, his shoulders drooping.

Organ Player looked like he'd rather die than lose to this nutcase, but he couldn't do anything about the physical damage. He tried to stand up, but his legs simply trembled, not letting him.

"Ugh. To… To be expected of Number Seven."

Without a means to fight, Organ Player no longer even had the stamina to escape.

Realizing this was the end of the road for him eventually, he looked up at Sogiita and said, "…Just one thing."

And then, a smile—a pure one, one you would never associate with a villain.

"Please, at the very least, finish me off with a single bombastic hit. Not that incredibly perfunctory 'awesome punch' or what have you—something real, a true beatdown that will make it actually *mean* something when I get blown away."

Upon hearing those words, Number Seven nodded quietly.

He slowly clenched his fist…

"Awesome *puuunch*."

"The hell?! I told you to stop doing th— *Arghhh?!*"

CHAPTER 5

What Is It the World Lacks?
First Friday of April

Brazil.

The emerging world power was said to have the third-largest economic growth in the world, after China and India, but that blessing hadn't yet reached the whole of the nation. Even in its capital, Rio de Janeiro, the gap between the rich and poor was immediately apparent, as though human lives had been cleanly divided along invisible lines.

On one street corner of that Brazilian metropolis, one that had a notably shadowy impression, stood an Asian man. He was in his mid- to late thirties and was quite tall, and he had a handsome face. His appearance would have stood out like a sore thumb in the country he'd been born in, but in this one, he felt like it buried him in the crowds.

But he wasn't someone you might think to approach.

He seemed to be fairly well-off, but he didn't give off the impression of a mindless sightseer. To begin with, he had the sort of slick looks that didn't stand out on this kind of back road. Who knew what kind of trouble one would get into if they approached him carelessly?

"Oh, what is this, miss?" the man said into the dark. "You sure have something good on your hands there."

No response. But he could tell that she'd shifted. The sunlight almost never reached this spot, but silhouettes were still visible, if nothing else. Standing there was a girl with light brown skin and Latino features.

Seemingly lacking any composure, she glared at the man. "What the hell do you want? Aren't you a little old to be snatching allowances?"

"You've got a gun in that handbag, don't you?" the man retorted simply.

This time, the girl's shoulders really gave a start. And after that, they froze solid.

Ignoring this, the man continued lightly, almost as if humming a song. "Not simple suicide, then—you plan to take someone with you. And not a family member or lover. It's someone you hate. Usually, that means killing a debt collector or something to make it easier for your family. Am I right?"

"...How do you know that?"

"You might not believe it, but I've got an eye for this sort of thing," the man said, pointing to his right eye and flashing her a mischievous look. "Let's have a chat. Unfortunately, now that I've realized you're out to kill, I'll have to stop you, or people might decide I'm aiding and abetting a murder. And this might actually work out in your favor, too."

"Who are you?"

"Hmm. Misaka. Tabigake Misaka."

Once the Asian introduced himself as Misaka, it was the girl's turn to introduce herself. She said that her name was Inés. It could have been a fake name, but Misaka's gut told him that was unlikely. To be blunt, Inés didn't currently have the capacity to do something so calculating.

"Are you Japanese? What do you do as a job? And do you have money?"

"My job... Well, I guess you could call me an integration consultant. No money, if that's what you're after. My job is creating money, not saving it up. I am technically rewarded, but my wife is in charge of my wallet. I get so little of it to use that I have to seriously worry about ditching drinking altogether."

"You're useless."

"So quick to cut me down. But it's too early to give up. You might find a chance to get out of this quagmire you're in by talking to me. In fact, I know of several people who *have* carved out their own paths in life by doing just that."

"?"

"My job is to show what the world lacks."

"What are you talking about?"

"Well, broadly speaking, I show people new business opportunities. If they implement the ideas I suggest in the right way, they can become presidents of whole companies. Tickled pink, on a bed of bills—"

"That's stupid," interrupted Inés. She turned to look around, then pointed at a corner where consumer electronic garbage had accumulated in a pile. "The only stuff we got in this town is trash. Rio de Janeiro has a lot of different things, but those are the only kind we can have. Get it? We don't even have the money to pay garbagemen to pick up the trash around here, so collection gets really backed up, too. Even if there was a chance, all we can do is twiddle our thumbs. That's what it means to be poor. Rich people don't want us turning it around on them right now. They even steal our chances away."

"Excuses? Excuses certainly feel good. The highest form of entertainment, in my opinion. What's yours? The government? Society? The environment you were born into?"

"What would you know anyway?" Inés didn't lose her cool at even that; her quiet anger simply simmered within her. "I'm young and don't have any schooling. The only thing someone like me can do is wipe down car windows, and I only get scraps for that. What am I supposed to do with that? It's not even enough to pay interest on our loan. It's barely enough to tip the men who come to collect."

"That isn't true," said Misaka simply, even seeing the girl's resigned expression. "Your chance might be surprisingly close at hand. You just don't see it." He paused. "Hey, just a question for you. You're not thinking I'm some kind of saint bursting with goodwill and an obsessively charitable mindset, are you? I have my own goals, so you don't have to worry about that. I've thought it all through. I'm not trying to give you random, unhelpful advice, sip my tea, and pat myself on the back for it. I'm the type who personally takes care of the people he wants to make use of."

"A goal? Are you saying you're going to make love to a kid or something to let her make money?"

"A charming invitation, but unfortunately that would be rude to my wife, and I can't help but remember my daughter, who is about your age."

"Then what else do you want me to do? You can't possibly mean there's some kind of chance in a place with illegally dumped bulk trash. That would be crazy."

"Oh, but it's not."

"?"

"I'll let you in on a secret—I'm here on a request from a certain person. He wants me to do something about unlawful dumping in Brazil. That means I *have* to do something about it. Real pain in the butt, but it's my job."

"That's stupid. And impossible. What, are you going to put up some signs telling people to stop littering? No one will follow that. People who litter aren't doing it because they want to. They know it's wrong, but that doesn't make illegal dumping go away. We just don't have the money to take care of it the right way."

"Is that really true?" Misaka grinned. "Like I said, my job is to show what the world lacks. And this little slum world—plagued with its illegal dumping of consumer appliance trash and your crippling poverty—what does it lack? Yes, Inés, if you know the answer, then please raise your hand."

"It's pretty obvious." Inés sighed, annoyed, answering without wasting a second, "Money."

"Bingo."

"...So that was how you encountered the Asian calling himself a consultant?"

"Well, yes. At first, I wasn't sure whether to believe him, either. But I decided the possibility was worth taking the chance. Better that than diving into a lair of debt collectors with mafia connections with nothing but a gun anyway."

Inés was currently in the lounge of what was probably the most expensive hotel in Rio de Janeiro. A journalist, carrying recording equipment, was clad in a brand-name outfit, but Inés was wearing what she always did. Still, nobody was going to complain about that.

The journalist went on. "Even so, retrieving the rare metals in the bases of consumer electronic garbage is quite a substantial business to start up."

"Well, everybody's always known that integrated circuits and chips and the like had trace amounts of pure gold in them. Nobody did it because it was too much trouble to reclaim anything worthwhile, but we didn't have any other options. We weren't after loftier goals."

In the very beginning, there weren't any machines or workshops. The entire operation relied on manual labor to pry off the plastic on integrated circuits, then patiently collect the gold, which was like fluffy lint. Once there was enough that it would fill about a lunch box, they would finally trade it in for paper bills. With those funds, tools to more efficiently extract the rare metals were finally obtainable, which helped earn even more money… It hadn't taken very long for the whole thing to balloon into something one could officially call an "enterprise." It hadn't even been a year since that day.

"One of the big hurdles was programming a machine arm for properly prying off the lids of all the different kinds of integrated circuits, but when we hit upon the idea of using ultrasonic waves to measure their sizes, it was pretty easy."

"Ultrasonic waves…?"

"What, didn't think a brat who never finished school could have come up with that? If I set my mind to it, stuff like that comes pretty easy."

Large swathes of Rio de Janeiro's population suffered from severe income gaps. But on the flip side, that meant once a proper foundation was finally laid down, steady development and growth were bound to follow. Inés was a perfect example of that.

"Reports are saying that illegal dumping all over Brazil, not even in just Rio de Janeiro, has fallen by over seventy percent. Word is that the Minister of the Environment will be giving you a commendation soon."

"People litter because it's cheaper. If people are driven to that, they won't have time to listen to things about morals and the belief that humans are fundamentally good. The best way to stop them from doing the wrong thing is to offer them a means of making money."

"And by telling people that trash is money, you've changed the entire world's perspective on it."

"……" Inés fell silent for a moment at the comment.

The man who called himself Misaka—was that what he'd been after?

The world could change.

And it *would*, so long as people who wanted to change it stood up and did something.

The important thing was just to start acting.

Was it his job to give people the power to do that?

"Next, we're going to use our funds to look for more efficient ways to reuse and recycle plastic and metals such as iron and steel. If we succeed at that venture, consumer electronics trash will turn into almost one hundred percent useful materials."

"That does sound promising. I've been hoping for a story about a bright view on the future," said the journalist, trying to please her.

Inés mostly ignored this, and suddenly she remembered what Tabigake Misaka had asked her.

…What is it the world lacks?

He was probably still fighting against the world.

Because according to him, that was his job.

CHAPTER 6

Gossip and Real Talk at the Salon

Fourth Friday of April

Chirp-chirp, came an electronic noise.

It was the automatic door's chime going off several times.

"Hmm? Oh, a customer."

"…Yeah, so peel your eyes away from that game, stupid shopkeeper. I'll traumatize you until the words *service industry* are seared into your mind."

The twin-tailed brunette, a young lady by the name of Kuroko Shirai, spoke under her breath. She leveled a glare at the beautician who was utterly devoid of enthusiasm as soon as she stepped into the place. Several young men on the staff immediately came out from the back and began bowing profusely to Shirai in apology.

Why on earth are the newbies who just got hired three months ago more worried about the shop than he is? Shirai was appalled, but the manager was good at what he did, so she couldn't complain too much. She entered a space partitioned off by a cloth screen, like in the nurse's office, then was led to a chair that looked like it was from a *dentist's* office. That's where she sat down.

The unenthused manager went around behind Shirai, his fingers—unusually slender for a man—undoing the ribbons tying her hair up.

The manager, Michibata Sakashima, rubbed his beard for a few moments, then said, "I've been hooked on different ways to use curling irons recently. How about a fourteen-loop ultra-drill style

I've been testing? Want me to croissant it up, just to see? You can be overbearing sometimes, so I think it would be perfect on you: mademoiselle-style vertical rolls."

"I've always had frizzy hair. Stow the sleep talk, clean up the ends, and give me a straight perm."

"Right... An Afro, was it?"

"I *said*, straight perm!!" shouted Shirai, her eyes nearly popping out when Sakashima tried to put a hemispherical bowl machine on her head.

"Okay, okay, jeez, so boring," muttered Sakashima. "I'll clean up the ends first." He took out a pair of thin-bladed scissors, then said, "You must have it as rough as the rest of us, Shirai."

"What do you mean?"

"Tokiwadai Middle School is an elite supernatural Ability Development academy. You need your teacher's permission to pick out a place to get your hair cut, don't you? Not that I'm not grateful, mind you—getting chosen by the school like this has been earning me money hand over fist. But it must be pretty stifling for the students."

"Well, if I complained about that, I'd have to complain about a million other things. Hair and blood are the archetypical bundles of genetic samples. They wouldn't be able to bear it if our DNA maps were secretly harvested and analyzed."

"Hmm."

Holding several metal combs in his left hand, each with different tooth sizes, the manager looked up. Countless cameras, big and small, looked back at him. The excessive number of them had not been installed by a security agency but Tokiwadai Middle School.

Sakashima pinched a tuft of Shirai's hair between his fingers and said, "Come to think of it, there was talk about them getting some grants to help with their teleportation Ability Development research. It must not be popular with scholars, having to think in terms of eleven-dimensional coordinate relationships."

"...It's mostly quantum theory when you get to eleven dimensions. Schrödinger-level stuff. But it's not that. It's just that there aren't many teleport espers, and the higher-ups seem to think it's some kind of crisis. I don't know why they don't get it—some talents more easily manifest in espers than others, that's all."

"That's a mystery in itself. First graders don't get electives, right? They all go through the same curriculum, but some of them start shooting fire or wind, branching out into all sorts of abilities."

As they continued their conversation, Sakashima trimmed Shirai's hair back about five millimeters. The tips of his blades, positioned at exactly the right angles, cut through the hair cleanly without destroying any cells.

"I do have to wonder why they bother developing all these supernatural abilities, though."

"…I'd rather you not deny Academy City's most fundamental reason for existence."

"I mean, I can understand it has its draws. But it makes me think whoever's behind it has dreams of immortality, or world conquest, or high offices in politics." Michibata cracked his neck a few times, still snipping away with the scissors. "I have to wonder if students like you would be mentioned in ability-related texts. There was that Cold War thing a while back—supernatural Ability Development was all the rage back then, too. The U.S. and the Soviets were throwing their budget into it just to try and one-up the other, like children… I mean, it ended in failure, but still."

"You mean the Stargate project, right?"

"Oh? You know it?" came his befuddled voice.

Shirai sighed. "We learned about it in history class. They did all these grand experiments following theories that were way off the mark. And they didn't even know what result values might indicate success or failure. It was a bunch of bourgeois scientists gobbling up the national budget while fumbling around in the dark. Or something like that."

"Hmm. On the surface of things, the project was for finding military uses for psychics, but I wonder if it was *actually* for something else. I can't help but think personal, emotional, subjective motives were at work. A really lame desire of some kind—like someone in love with the idea of *special people* or *chosen ones*," said Sakashima as he ran a comb through Shirai's hair and pinched another tuft.

Shirai hated to admit it, but the sensation didn't feel half bad.

"...But what *was* it, I wonder?" continued Sakashima.

"What was what?"

"Oh, I mean, the Cold War–era psychic power development. The only ones who succeeded at researching supernatural powers to the point they were usable was Japan's Academy City. But that leaves the question of where the U.S. and Soviets got their hands on samples of psychics."

"If they said there were zero successes, they'd lose authority over the people paying taxes for it. They were probably just bluffing."

"But you see things every once in a while—you know, on TV and stuff. Former elite investigators and the like taking on unresolved incidents. I doubt *everything* is a bluff. At the very least, if nobody gave eyewitness testimony to having seen something like that, they'd never have wanted to try and make it themselves in the first place."

"...Have you heard of the fraud of alchemy in the Middle Ages? Do you think the royals and aristocrats and everyone else believed alchemy was real because they'd seen the actual thing?"

"Ugh. Unfortunately for you, I believe in alchemy—and UFOs and the New Jersey Devil."

"......" Shirai flashed him an appalled look. The guy wasn't about to claim fast-food chain hamburgers had earthworm meat in them, was he? "What, then? Are you saying some of Academy City's technological information was leaked to the U.S. and Russia during the Cold War?"

"The Soviet Union, you mean. And no, that couldn't have happened. Academy City's technological level is twenty or thirty years ahead of the rest of the world. Even if literally all of its information was leaked, they wouldn't have the technology to break our more advanced encryption, so there'd be nothing they could do. I doubt they could have gotten there that way."

"Supercomputers on the outside at the time couldn't even run the latest portable video games," added Sakashima with a laugh. "They wouldn't have been able to read an Academy City disc if we'd placed it right in front of them, much less decrypt anything."

"Then what are you trying to get at?"

"Well, Shirai, haven't you heard about Uncut Gems?"

"……"

"Oh, does it make you angry?"

"Of course it does. Scientists make us polish our abilities day in, day out, using electrodes and drugs, delivering shocks to our brains, and even resorting to hypnotic suggestions—and then you bring *that* up."

"I figure it's only the difference between man-made diamonds and natural ones," said Sakashima, working his scissors along her bangs. "As long as we can consistently recreate a specific phenomenon artificially, then assuming the right factors occur in the natural world to make an environment exactly the same as one of our research facilities, the same phenomenon should happen even without human assistance. If the diamond example doesn't suit your fancy, maybe an analogy with Tasers and lightning is more to your liking?"

"It's all a theory," countered Shirai, unamused. "I've never seen one in the wild. And even if they do exist, samples must be extremely rare. So rare they'd be mistaken for errors in the data, and you'd get a display that returns a grand total of zero."

"Hmm." Sakashima narrowed his eyes and gave a pleasant smile.

Suddenly, he stopped his scissors. He said, as if to challenge his customer: "Lightning *does* strike fairly frequently, you know."

"It hitting you in the *head* is a much less common occurrence, though."

CHAPTER 7
A Certain Mastermind's Preparations and Cleanup

Second Friday of May

It was just a quick stop in the city of Milan.

And then an entire human trafficking ring got destroyed.

"Yes, I understand that, but…"

The tall woman standing in the front entrance, Sylvia, looked at the man with questioning eyes. More specifically, she looked behind the man—behind Ollerus.

"Who is that behind you?" she asked.

"I—I mean, you know. I was only planning on busting the ring and feeling real good about myself, but then a whole crowd of kids came out the back, and… If I'd left them there, someone else might have kidnapped them instead, so I guess what I'm trying to say is—"

"You brought them with you?"

"Erk."

"You took almost a hundred children back home with you? What are you, the Pied Piper of Hamelin?"

Ollerus found himself unable to answer Sylvia's question.

For a few moments, there was silence.

Then, Sylvia sighed and closed the front door.

"Hey!! Wait, wait!! This was the best solution!! It's not like I'm going to ask you to renovate the apartment into a school (specifically a boarding school) right this instant!! It's only until we can find them foster parents!!"

"Get rid of them."

"That's not a solution!! How could I do that to them, you cold-blooded woman?! You sound like someone's mom telling them to get rid of an animal! Lend a hand to those in need—it's a fundamental law of the world!!"

"Why, you dusty fallen noble... If that was true, then nobody would have any problems, now *would* they?!"

The front door slammed open wide, striking Ollerus directly and sending him flying away like in a karate movie.

Meanwhile, Sylvia put her hands on her hips and seethed. "You're acting so high-and-mighty and selfish, but how exactly do you plan on taking care of them?! Eh?! All you do is make promises you can't keep! Get over here!! I will tie you up with ropes and then make you straddle the roof of the doghouse!! I will physically show you what it means to anger this *bonne dame*!!"

"Heegyaaaahhhhhhh?! A DIY wooden horse?!"

Not long after, Ollerus's thighs were splayed out on the quaint lawn in front of the apartment. In any case, the nearly hundred kids couldn't be left to their own devices, so for now Sylvia invited them into the apartment building.

After Sylvia and the mass of children had disappeared into the building, one child pattered up to Ollerus, who had been left there after being forced to uncomfortably ride atop the doghouse beside the front entrance.

The girl said, "I want to repay you."

"Heh... Heh-heh-heh. I didn't save you all because I was looking for that type of reward."

The girl looked hard at Ollerus riding the doghouse. "...Will you be okay like that, then?"

"Not what I meant," declared Ollerus. "In the end, it's just that it wouldn't mean anything."

"?"

"I'm honored you look up to me, but it's misplaced admiration. Tying you up and forcing you to do manual labor wouldn't be any different from the human trafficking business. That's not what I'm searching for."

"But I still want to repay you."

"If you're serious about it, then I want you to try and attain fulfilling happiness with your own hands," said Ollerus, his face the picture of seriousness, spread-eagled as he was over the doghouse.

"I saved you even though I knew Sylvia would give me a thrashing. It's only natural I'd want you to be happy. Demanding anything else of you wouldn't be right."

Even though he said that to her, she still wanted to repay him.

She couldn't get rid of the murk in her heart now that she owed him a debt.

To properly thank Ollerus in a way he'd appreciate, she first needed to know who the person named Ollerus was.

The next person the girl approached was Sylvia. She—having already apologized profusely to the landlord and was currently racking her brain, wondering how she was going to cook food for a hundred and what she was even going to do about blankets and sleeping space—answered the girl's question.

"He's a man who should have become a magic god."

"?"

"I don't mean a real god or anything—a magic god is a person who has set foot into God's domain through mastery over sorcery." Sylvia's tone was casual and slow. "Any normal person could easily die just from reading so many original copies of grimoires, but for him, the bigger problem was that the power wielded by magic gods is far too specialized. You can have the prerequisite knowledge, but all that information is pointless without the energy to put it into practice. In the end, he only barely scraped it together in that regard by using a treatise on Hliðskjálf while refining his life force into mana for conversion into that special power.

"If someone *could* use a magic god's power with only a normal level of mana, they'd be a literal monster," added Sylvia.

Though the girl felt like Sylvia had tried to explain it to her in an easy-to-understand way, she actually understood nothing at all.

Sylvia watched the girl's face, then sighed. "Basically, it's like a wonderful job that everyone dreams of having. Like being in the major leagues or representing the nation in the World Cup."

"...He was *supposed* to become one?"

"Yeah, he was, that idiot," said Sylvia, spitting out the words like they were dirt that had gotten into her mouth. "...Ollerus had a chance that only comes around once every ten thousand years, if that. He knew if he let the chance go, he might never get another one. And what do you think he did? It wasn't even a *person* he saved. He was running all around the city to save this injured kitten, looking for an animal hospital, and during that time, he turned his back on the opportunity."

"......"

"He should've just gone for it. He slipped up like an idiot, though, and now he spends his days getting wrapped up in crisis after crisis... He really *is* an idiot. Or maybe I should call him *emotional*. He's not perfect. Occasionally, he'll remember it, and he'll sob to himself long into the night."

Sylvia exhaled.

Then she continued, "It's just that he talks about it a certain way."

"What does he say?"

"He says he's regretted it ever since then, and if he was put in the same situation again, there's no guarantee he would be able to do the same thing. But he says he truly thought, at the time, that what he did was the right thing to do."

"......"

"Anyway, that's the long and short of it. He's fundamentally an idiot. And after a while of watching him, I ended up protecting him and started thinking like an idiot myself. That's why we're stuck here and not going back to the United Kingdom."

Once the children had fallen asleep while wrapped in a hundred blankets Sylvia had somehow procured, Sylvia collapsed over the table, looking crushed under the weight of exhaustion. And then she started cursing someone.

"…I'm going to let you taste the fear of lacquer all over your body after this."

"Eek?! Getting spread-eagled over a wooden horse is one thing, but hellish itchiness is terrifying in its own right, you know!"

"Well, you'll just have to put up with it until we can hand these kids over to the nearby church… About one week, tops. It'll be itchy every day, but it's a good chance to train your mind."

"Oh, damn!! Are you gonna leave it painted all over me?!"

"More importantly, you found the signs?"

"Yeah, er. Matches the list. Only a few of them, though. As I thought, that human trafficking group was dealing in people with all sorts of special traits, major and minor."

"…Which means it's been proven, then."

"Mm," mumbled Ollerus, stretching. "Looks like it's going to get busy again."

I want to repay you, said the girl.

Time, however, would not wait.

The man who should have become a magic god left town the very next day and never came back.

CHAPTER 8
Kunoichi Always Appear Unannounced
Fourth Friday of May

...Man. I wonder why Komaba got all serious and said I'd be Skill-Out's leader if anything happened to him.

Shiage Hamazura, Academy City delinquent, was, as customary, wielding several needles as he engaged in melee combat with the lock on the door of a sports car.

"...Sir Hamazura."

"Hmm?" Hamazura stopped his work and looked here and there, suddenly hearing a woman's voice. But there was nobody near this sports car parked on the road.

Guess I'm hearing things, thought Hamazura, beginning to clack the needles around again.

"...Sir Hamazura."

What?! Some kind of weird fountain fairy?! Hamazura thought, quivering with fear. *She's not gonna do that crazy thing where water spouts out of a nearby manhole and she asks, "Was the sports car you dropped this gold one or this silver one?" or anything, right?!*

"Sir Hamazura!!"

Suddenly, a face popped out from underneath the vehicle like a mechanic.

"H-huh?! The sports car I dropped was just a normal one!! Wait—crap! I didn't drop anything to begin with! I'm not an honest person at all!!"

"?" said the mysterious figure as it wriggled out.

It was a girl.

She was technically wearing a yukata, but she certainly didn't give off the impression of being a classical Japanese woman. She had black hair at least, but there was some brown speckling around her bangs, and she had a rainbow of traditional hair ornaments with beads on them. Her nails on both hands were covered in glaring nail art. She had a lace glove on one of her arms, too. Her footwear, while similar to geta, were actually just completely regular sandals, the kind with the thin straps winding all the way up to the knees. And for whatever reason, something that looked like a metal shackle was attached to only one of her ankles.

...In fact, even the yukata she wore was a bright yellow mini-yukata, the kind that would make a lot of stubborn old craftsmen froth at the mouth. Her dazzling thighs were exposed, and for some reason, the left sleeve was missing, and her arm was bare up to the shoulder. Her wide-width obi was, for some reason, made of a see-through material, and that portion of the underlying fabric itself was transparent to match, which managed to let her show her navel even though she was wearing a yukata. She had two thin leather belts wrapped around the obi, too, and to top it all off, she was adorned in awfully long chains.

Even Hamazura, a bargain-bin delinquent who was already plenty ostentatious, couldn't help but judge her outfit as *super* gaudy. But the thing was, the cloth used in her yukata was surprisingly high quality. It made it feel like even more of a waste.

...If I'm getting aggravated over that outfit, I guess I have more of my Japanese spirit left than I thought.

He thought that only came out during the Olympics or the World Cup—it shocked him that it would show up for something so negative.

But this wasn't the time for him to be awakening a weird, new-found sense of love of his homeland. "Er, Kuruwa, was it? If you're looking for Hanzou, I haven't seen him."

"Mgh. I've yielded the initiative. If you know not of his where-abouts, Sir Hamazura, then where could Lord Hanzou be...?"

"......"

It wasn't just her clothing—the way she talked was weird, too. *Still, I guess anything goes if you've got a huge rack.*

…No, more importantly, Hamazura didn't know much at all about this Kuruwa girl. She seemed to have been hanging around his bad friend Hanzou for quite some time now. Just recently, only about a week ago, while Hamazura was in a hideout garage prying open the door of a safe he and Hanzou had stolen together, he'd run into Kuruwa by pure coincidence; she'd been searching for Hanzou. That was all.

It seemed Hanzou was avoiding her; every time he'd throw her off his scent, Kuruwa would come to either Hamazura like this or his other partner in crime, Ritoku Komaba, and ask about Hanzou.

Damn it, Hanzou. Her boobs are so big, too.

Hamazura groaned softly in thought as he stared at the tightly wrapped bulges in her thin summer yukata. Still, looking at her outfit—which Kuruwa had customized almost beyond recognition—he couldn't help but think it seemed less of a kimono and more a kunoichi's uniform or something.

And then, Hamazura thought, *Hmm?*

A kunoichi.

A female ninja.

Hanzou, being chased by a ninja.

Hanzou.

"Ah-ha-ha-ha. Hattori Hanzou!" he muttered in amusement without meaning to—then figured that couldn't possibly be true. Was he stupid? Hattori Hanzou wasn't real! He turned back to the sports car, fully intending to resume his battle with the lock, when…

"O-oh-no-no-no-no-no-no-no, I… I have to get rid of Sir Hamazura now?!"

"*Gnrgh?!* Such an obvious plot twist, and yet for a ninja, you reacted so stupidly!! W-wait, are you serious? Is Hanzou, like, the descendant of near-future shinobi warriors who survived until the present day or something?!"

Seeing as how Kuruwa started visibly fidgeting and panicking, that did indeed seem to be the case... But hold on, a descendant of ninjas? Hanzou didn't know how to use some crazy ninja techniques or anything, did he? Strange images floated into Hamazura's mind.

"But wait," he said. "Why would a kunoichi be chasing him?"

"Urk?!"

"If Hanzou is from the Hattori clan, then what clan are you from, Kuruwa?"

"Uuurk?!"

"Hattori Hanzou, huh—just hearing those two names makes him sound like an ultra-important person. I bet there's some kind of conspiracy in one of the shinobi clans, and now Hanzou is gonna charge into a battle of awesome proportions!!" Hamazura snapped his fingers, imagining his friend in danger, as if it had absolutely nothing to do with him.

Kuruwa, however, her whole body sweating and her eyes somehow uncertain, said, "...Now that you know too much, I truly cannot allow you to escape alive...!!"

"No way!! Are your world's conspiracies really that cliché?!"

Hamazura buried his face in his hands, but Kuruwa really seemed to be freaking out. As he was wondering if he should just give up on the sports car and dash away, Kuruwa pulled something out of her right sleeve—which, unlike her left, was so long only her fingertips poked out of it. It was a black, metallic object.

According to Kuruwa's very confident explanation...

"Ta-daa! It's a gun!! Prepare thyself, Sir Hamazuraaaaa!!"

"Huh...?"

"Wh-why do you seem so utterly disappointed?! This is a serious development!! Please approach this with an open mind! Come hither—hither!!"

"I mean, uh, you're a ninja, right...? Are guns, like...kosher?"

Seeing Hamazura awash with extraordinary disappointment, the modern kunoichi Kuruwa began to hastily explain herself, as though a little seed of guilt had sprouted in her mind.

"Shinobi have always armed themselves with the latest weaponry!

It's totally A-OK!! Even the veteran shinobi who supported the world from the Sengoku to the Edo would camouflage matchlocks within the likes of staves or pillboxes!! So it's totally A! O! K!!"

"That's not what I meant. I don't give a rat's ass about history or whatever; it's all bullshit anyway. Just stop destroying my dreams!! I want to see a smoke cloud and a whole bunch of shadow clones!! I'm just sick of this now! I admit it!! I was a fool for clinging to such strange preconceptions!! I guess I'll go over to the riverbank and cry for a while!!"

"W-wait!! Please hold!! Ahhh, please, I implore you to not run away with such sadness in your eyes!!"

There Hamazura and Kuruwa were, starting to act like a couple on the brink of divorce. *Damn, I wanted to use that excuse to run away,* thought Hamazura, cursing to himself.

Kuruwa, for her part, didn't appear to notice Hamazura's intentions. She seemed to have completely forgotten about her initial objective of finding Hanzou, to boot. "A-a-a-all right! I shall show you something special! Look—this nice young lady is about to show you a genuine ninja technique!!"

"...Really? You're just saying that, right?"

"I'm telling the truth!! Real, bona fide secret ninja arts!! I—I must say, Sir Hamazura, you are a lucky one—chances such as these do not come often!!"

Kuruwa's face wore the kind of half-smiling, half-teary-eyed expression that only came to truly desperate people. *Wait, am I actually gonna get to see some real ninja shit?* thought Hamazura, his interest slightly piqued. Kuruwa motioned for him to follow her, and then she wandered into an alley.

"Mm-hmm—maybe it really is a secret ninja move. Guess you can't do it in public?"

"Well, not exactly, but… Well, it's embarrassing, so…"

"Huh?"

Then came the rustling of fabric.

What lay before him was…

"Huh—? Wait, hold on. What the heck are you doing?!"

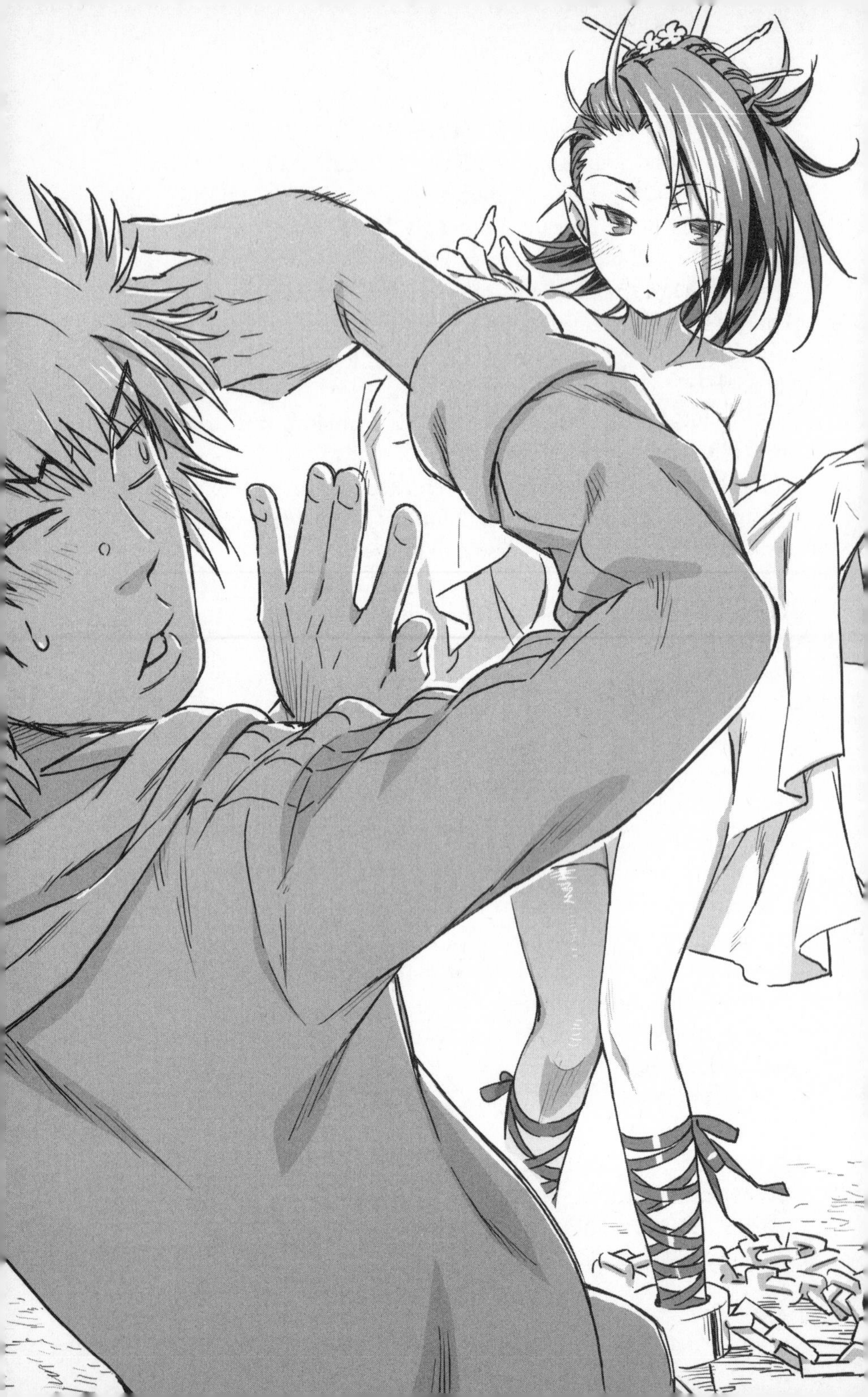

"Um, well—you *did* tell me to show you a kunoichi art, Sir Hamazura."

"Yeah, but *that's* not what I meant!! Hey—hey! I can see everything, you know! You idiot, everything's visible!! Gwah—come on!! Father doesn't approve of this! And why are you wiggling your hips like that—what exactly are you trying to do?!"

"What do you mean? I'm simply taking this here and doing this, then this, and..."

"Waaahhh?! I—this—this is...!! You're coming at me with *that* angle?! This isn't even just about being able to see anymore, it's—*garrghh*, wah, *waaaaaaaaaaaaahhhhhhhhhhhhhhhhhhhhh?!*"

"Hi-yah! You're wide open! ☆"

By the time Hamazura thought, *Huh?* it was too late.

With a dull *ka-thump*, he hit the ground.

CHAPTER 9
Electrons Need No Earthly Relationships
Second Friday of June

That's where the Goalkeeper is. And it's my job to fight them.

Kihan Kuyama was a hacker.

The type of hacker who didn't particularly care about the differences between the white-hats and black-hats or the kinds that tended to show up in fiction for a while. A simpler name for him might have been Internet criminal. The first time Kuyama had touched a computer had been in the earlier half of elementary school. He'd been randomly pressing keys and coincidentally gotten past a staff member's password lock. Ever since then, it had been a fixation of his to find the holes in computer systems. He'd researched all sorts of things after that, and by the time he got to high school, he'd already earned himself that strange title.

Around here, maybe?

Kuyama was sitting in a corner of an utterly unextraordinary open café that had a wireless LAN hot spot. He never made the mistake of letting an opponent trace him, and even if anyone tried, he always made sure to spoof his source address, so nine times out of ten it wouldn't be an issue. Still, he never felt like going to battle in his own home.

A waitress approached with a smile; Kuyama put in an offhand order as he took out a laptop. This was his weapon. On the outside, it seemed like a cheap model from a common manufacturer, but on the inside lay something entirely different; he'd replaced everything, starting from the machine's very foundation. Even so, all Academy City computers were preset with a security rank—D, C, B, A, or S—for that specific device, as well as something like a serial number. No matter how he spoofed his address, he'd had to do something about that number—it was embedded directly in the circuitry—or else the danger of them discovering his identity skyrocketed.

I'm actually nervous. That's unusual, he thought, plugging in a wireless card—separate from the one already inside the laptop. *Makes sense, though. I'm about to break into the Goalkeeper's very own computer system.*

He was operating less on information and more on an urban legend.

Among those who kept the peace in Academy City was an incredibly skilled hacker. Whoever they were, their abilities were outstanding, and the security system they'd created using all the knowledge and skills at their disposal was apparently one of the top ten tightest in the whole city. The General Board chairperson didn't trust their abilities, however, and they ended up not adopting it for use in public systems. That created an odd setup where the small little office that hacker worked in had defenses several times tougher than even the data banks that managed information for all of Academy City.

He'd thought it was a joke.

This hacker world had been created by those with unknown faces and names. Infestations of groundless information were the norm, not the exception—always seeking to stir up gossip or to make the mastermind seem bigger and better than they were.

But the vague rumors had lined up with concrete evidence.

Within the past week, several hackers Kuyama knew had been arrested. And yes, every single one of them had been attempting to break into a *certain system*.

He'd never actually met any of them for real, but he *did* have a handle on their abilities. He'd had chats with them about how to illegally modify their stats in online games before. Considering their skills, he doubted they'd *all* messed up trying to get into some trivial system, like one belonging to Anti-Skill or Judgment.

Something was up.

And that thing was, in all likelihood, the Goalkeeper.

I'm not trying to steal information or anything. And it's not that the so-called Goalkeeper rubs me the wrong way, either.

Academy City regulations stated that crimes related to electronic communication carried a maximum of twenty years' imprisonment with hard labor or a fine of up to fifty million yen. The risks of intrusion for no reason were certainly not low, but...

Still, my master key needs to work on everything. As soon as there's a door that I can't open, the master key is as good as garbage.

He wasn't exactly doing this because he hated to lose—it was to tear off a label unfairly applied to him.

He sought freedom, and he wouldn't let anything stand in his way, no matter how small.

And that was what moved Kihan Kuyama, the hacker who didn't seek reward.

The first thing Kuyama did was not spoof his ID using some obscure method, nor was it to undo password lock screens with incredibly fast keystrokes.

The first order of business was simply setting up his shortcut keys.

Maybe I'll go with Preset 3 today—4 or 1 might be good, too.

He consulted his list of on-hand hacking programs to select the ones he'd use. After that, he assigned them all at once to the leftover keys on his keyboard, setting it up so that he could boot up any of them he wanted with a single keystroke.

What Kuyama was doing was akin to saving certain frequently used chat patterns for online games, such as "heal pls" or "let's pull back," in advance, so that he only had to press a few buttons to say them. There wasn't much point to laboring over every single character, and most importantly, that would prevent quick reaction times.

The only flaw was if he needed any commands that he *hadn't* set up in advance, he'd need to switch to doing things manually and typing out commands. It was best to consider most of those unusable in real world conditions. Because of that, he had to take into account the security level of what he was hacking, as well as what he'd need to do once inside, and from that, he put together the most optimal key setup he could.

After all, the Goalkeeper's skill is an unknown variable. Throwing up a smoke screen should be the safest option. I hate to be too cautious and come off as scared, but I should probably assume this enemy deserves at least that much respect.

This moment, when he tried to get inside an enemy's head and set up a limited hand for himself, was what Kuyama lived for. Even more than the feeling he got after breaking into a system. It made him feel as though he were connected with someone he couldn't see on the other side of the Internet.

…Then, driving away that particular joy, he heard a nearby table clatter. Kuyama looked over there and saw some huge-chested woman wearing a green tracksuit sitting down at it.

"Phew… Aah, it's such a pain having to write reports. Hey, miss—does this place have wireless LAN? I don't wanna have to bother going all the way back to school to turn this in, yeah?"

…The hell is she?

It said right on the front door of the shop whether or not there was wireless LAN access. In fact, the very *thought* of her trying to submit an official report through the wireless LAN, where you had *no idea* who might intercept any kind of message, struck the hacker as unbelievably oblivious. And it didn't look like she'd taken proper precautions to mitigate risk like he did.

Amateur, he thought contemptuously as he sneered at all the casual dabblers in every field before he immersed himself in his work.

After getting most of his shortcuts set up, Kuyama finally set off on his rather illegal caper.

Still, hackers weren't exactly superhuman. All he was planning to do was run somewhat unique programs, which were made for developers, to use a normal search engine to find a certain website on the Internet.

A regular old internet browser popped up in the middle of his laptop monitor, with several windows that had lots of weird scrolling numbers and symbols arrayed around its periphery. Basically, it was only showing information you couldn't generally see on the surface—none of it was any more than what a computer always processed.

Kuyama knew firsthand that the main thing hackers possessed that others didn't was *knowledge*.

How much of the information hidden behind the scenes did most people understand? Those good at scooping up goldfish at festivals knew the trick to that. Hackers were much the same.

To repeat, hackers were not superhuman.

Under normal circumstances, all they did was bring the processing that happened under the hood to the surface.

All right, let's get started.

He'd found the system administered by the Goalkeeper.

It obviously wasn't made for regular people to view, but it had an interface; the likes of Anti-Skill and Judgment could use it to exchange information through the system. That was the route Kuyama used to infiltrate.

As soon as he gained access, there was a change in the windows with the scrolling numbers and symbols. Several rows of characters stood apart from the rest, colored in red, displaying multiple warning symbols.

Hmm! A redirect, eh?!

A redirect was a mechanism to automatically move anyone who accessed the website to another website, without their input. In many cases, the resulting website was something horrible, the kind where viewing it could give you a virus.

In this case, the destination was most likely something that would collect his personal information. Regulations prevented Anti-Skill and Judgment from creating systems for themselves that obtained personal information in violation of privacy laws; their main motive for the redirect was to purposely send the infiltrator somewhere outside their system and cook their goose, as it were.

This time, though, Kuyama's reflexes were faster.

He'd noticed the Goalkeeper's land mine before stepping on it. He slipped around it instead, smiling to himself.

This wasn't how a protector did things. A redirect to a malicious website? It was obvious if you thought about what a weapon like that was originally made for. This was clearly how a hacker would *attack* someone.

And if he could see their system, he could discern their character.

While employing a rather shrewd method in response, Kuyama's spirits began to soar with joy, as though this were a simple game— and he was winning.

And then, someone threw a wet blanket over him once again.

"Oh, here it is! It's right here—right here!!"

The shrill voice belonged to a girl. Annoyed, Kuyama looked in that direction and saw someone who looked like she was in middle school at a table across from the lady in the green tracksuit, who had since grown bored of writing her report and was collapsed face-first on the table. The girl seemed to have a lot of flower decorations on her head that stuck out in the corner of his vision. She seemed to be playing a multiplayer game.

"Phew! Speed is finally stabilized... Wait, something terrible happened before I knew it?!"

Clack-clack-clack-clack went the buttons as the girl furiously pressed them hard enough to break them. Offhandedly noting how the only problem with mounting his attacks outside his home was that he couldn't fully immerse himself due to distractions, Kuyama focused his attention back at his laptop screen.

*   *   *

Several more traps were waiting for him after that, too.

One made it look like he'd broken into the system, another put him into a protracted command loop, and yet another forced absolutely unreadable file types to open and give him errors. As Kuyama had predicted, they were all things a hacker would use for offense, and many of them surprised even him, a hacker by trade, with their ingenuity.

But he hadn't fallen for any of them yet. Dangerous rows of characters would be marked in colors before he ran straight into them, and Kuyama would divert around them to get even deeper in.

Have I won?

The moment he had that thought, something changed.

A small window suddenly appeared at the edge of the screen. In it was a single indifferent word: *disconnected*. Kuyama was dubious, but there was no issue with his wireless LAN environment. Something or someone on the Goalkeeper's side had, for some reason, cut the power.

Did they notice me?!

Kuyama glanced at several windows, but fortunately, it didn't seem like his personal information had been collected. What most likely happened was his target realizing someone had hacked into the system, but they hadn't figured out exactly who, so they forced a shutdown, deciding it was too dangerous to let him fish around any longer.

Even as he planted several misdirects, just in case, and made absolutely sure not to leave any trace of himself, there was no sense of triumph on Kuyama's face.

That was good timing. I guess that makes it a draw for today.

While he had done everything electronically from start to finish, the Goalkeeper had been forced to resort to the physical solution of shutting off the power. In other words, Kuyama's hacking skills had won out. And it all but proved the effectiveness of his master key.

And then it happened.

The realization dawned on him.

That simple *disconnected* message from earlier. It would have appeared on the Goalkeeper's system at the same time it had shown up on Kuyama's laptop. If you cut a tin can telephone by its string, *both* people would no longer be able to hear the other.

And the exact same thing would happen in that same second of that minute of that hour of that day of that month of that year.

So... If the Goalkeeper used the display time on the message that came up on *their* system to investigate, wouldn't they be able to get a precise hit on him?

"...?!" A cold sweat broke out all over Kuyama's face.

N-no, I already built a program to spoof my source address. They couldn't possibly identify me instantaneously...!!

So he thought anyway, but the store's surveillance cameras, as well as the multiple lenses on a security robot running on the road outside, had just taken perfect aim at him, as though they were snipers. And as the pièce de résistance, someone laid a hand on Kuyama's shoulder. He didn't need to turn around. It belonged to an Anti-Skill officer: one of those who protected peace in the city.

"That's a violation of the regulation preventing unlawful electronic information manipulation. I'm not *requesting* you to come with me. You understand, right?"

But Kuyama wasn't listening to the deep voice.

Not even close.

Wait. It hasn't even been three minutes since my connection dropped. Anti-Skill couldn't have gotten here that fast, even if they did pinpoint where I was. Which means...

They'd noticed he was here much earlier.

But then *when?* And where? And how?

Then, he heard a clatter. He looked that way and saw the girl, the one who'd been playing her game, getting out of her seat. The flower-adorned girl headed for the register with her bill and said, "Um, can I get a receipt please? Yes—please charge it to Kazari Uiharu, of Judgment."

She went for the receipt even though all she'd done was play her video game. But Kuyama's face twisted as though he'd been punched in the gut. He finally realized what she'd actually been holding.

That…that's…

A portable game console that could connect to the net.

It could use wireless LAN, so it could theoretically also run programs on the Internet.

But…

It was a more practical issue. Could she *seriously* have fought Kuyama's fully decked-out hacking system with nothing but *that*?

Come to think of it, when she got here, she said something about speed having stabilized and then something terrible having happened before she realized it. Could that mean she was—?

"Hey… Hey, you!!"

Kuyama unconsciously tried to go up to the girl, but the Anti-Skill officer must have thought he was trying to run away and pinned him. Squashed on the ground now, Kuyama still stared at that girl. She didn't turn around. Not even once.

There was no proof that girl with the flower ornament was the Goalkeeper.

The real one could have surprisingly been giggling at him on the other end of the connection now. Maybe the Goalkeeper was a friend of hers, and she'd just been cheering them on from the sidelines.

However.

The problem wasn't the girl, per se.

The Goalkeeper had been right before his eyes, yet he hadn't been able to discern her—he'd only caught wavering glimpses of her shadow.

He stared at her back—at the person who was infinitely close to black but still somehow gray—the one who danced, her tail just out of reach—

"She's a hacker…," moaned Kuyama as cuffs were snapped close around his hands behind him.

"A…a *real* hacker."

CHAPTER 10

To Accept or Deny a Night's Invitation
First Friday of July

I don't know if it's foehn winds or an El Niño or what, but summer in London is so freaking hot and so freaking humid and so freaking oppressive, and I think I'm going to just die it's so hot tonight.

"...Isn't there anything you could do about the way you talk, Tanaka?"

"Come on, man—it's hot as *hell* out here."

The words sounded like a new employee who had agreed, at length, to *only* take her earrings out, and Touya Kamijou was fed up with it. "*You're* the one who suggested we go out for a drink after our work was over, you know."

"I've only been bringing us to pub after pub and they all have cute girls in them, and every single time you stomp your foot and say, *Let's go somewhere else* or *I'd rather not* or *Let's not go there, either!*"

"...That's because you're not taking into account that I'm a married man. Or are you purposely trying to tear us apart because you can't stand someone else not being single like you?"

"Ugh. Says the man who shrewdly ran into a blond, wavy-haired schoolgirl on the street corner; the very same man who was holding that blind nun's hand to show her where to go and later tripped, immediately diving into the chest of that other sister with sausage curls. And just what was with that girl yesterday anyway? It might be July, but you can't go around wearing barely anything like that..."

"Well, she seemed to be drifting around near the station. I called out to her, thinking she might be lost. I wonder what that was all about? She must have a lot on her mind..."

Touya began muttering to himself, but Tanaka wasn't listening. In general, a single person would only get pissed off listening to Touya. How had a guy like him convinced such a young, beautiful woman to agree to be his wife?

"The whole point of going for a drink was because it's hot out," said Tanaka. "But now we're sweaty just from looking for a place to go! What's the point?"

"I don't care where we go at this point, so let's pick the next place we see."

"Hopefully, it's somewhere we can sit down to drink, at least."

Once they'd decided on an extremely random course, they wandered into a pub like a couple of sleepwalkers—and inside they found surprisingly good-tasting local black beer. As they were putting away some fried fish and drinking their hearts out, they suddenly found they were now a group of three, with the addition of some drunk person they didn't even know.

"I'm *telling* you, you can *try* shaying *Please shtop cutting down trees for the shake of the planet*, but if you don't cut them down you can't get a paycheck or protect your family. If you were shomeone like that, would *you* listen to shomeone shuddenly coming up and giving you a do-good-to-the-environment talk? Greed is what movesh people! Greed, I shay! What I mean isss, to protect the environment, you gotta shet up a way for people to protect their families *without* cutting down trees, you *freaking moron!!*"

"...Er, who were you again?"

"Hmm?? I'm Misaka—Tabigake Misaka. Mackerel really make the best fish fries, huh? It's a little off-putting with them catching sooo many widdle baby mackerels, but ish still good stuff!"

Introducing himself, Misaka reached a fork out for the fish fries Touya and Tanaka ordered. On the surface, he seemed like the sort of dandy gentleman who would fit perfectly in a high-class car painted black, but it seemed the alcohol in the local beer had made him very talkative.

"And another thing—all those Japanese people who *love* their wooden homes sooo much that they're shouting *Cut down more! Cut down more!* turn around and tell the workers in the Amazon that *you're doing the wrong thing, you know!* Do they even understand what they're saying?! Those idiots! How can you talk about sounding the alarms of global warming when you don't even change the settings on your air conditioners, much less turn them off, you fake Samaritans! And if you don't like it, then make a system where you can protect everyone by raising some trees, goddamn it!!"

"I, uh, Kamijou, what's going on with this guy? He reeks of alcohol."

"...By the by, what kind of work do you two do?"

"Well, we work for an office that prevents buyouts related to our parent company..."

"Oh, huh? A company president?! Wait, hold on—I'm a person who shows people what the world lacks. The Amazon is a little hot at the moment—would you mind listening to what I have to shay, hmm? Would you?"

As they went on and on making a ruckus, they eventually heard a sigh from a table deeper in the pub. Touya looked over there, wondering if they'd been too noisy, and saw a blond-haired, blue-eyed lady in a close-fitting suit. He didn't know whether she intended it, but the sight of her drinking alone in the dimly lit place and her weary expression seemed to make her somehow exude this pinkish aura.

Tanaka, who had been completely preoccupied with Misaka until now, suddenly bolted upright.

Before Touya could think, *Oh crap, it's that habit of his,* Tanaka said, "I'm going to talk to her! I'm going to, I swear I will!!"

"Don't bother," said Touya with a chuckle. "It's suicide."

Abruptly, Misaka countered, "Actually, with her, it might work."

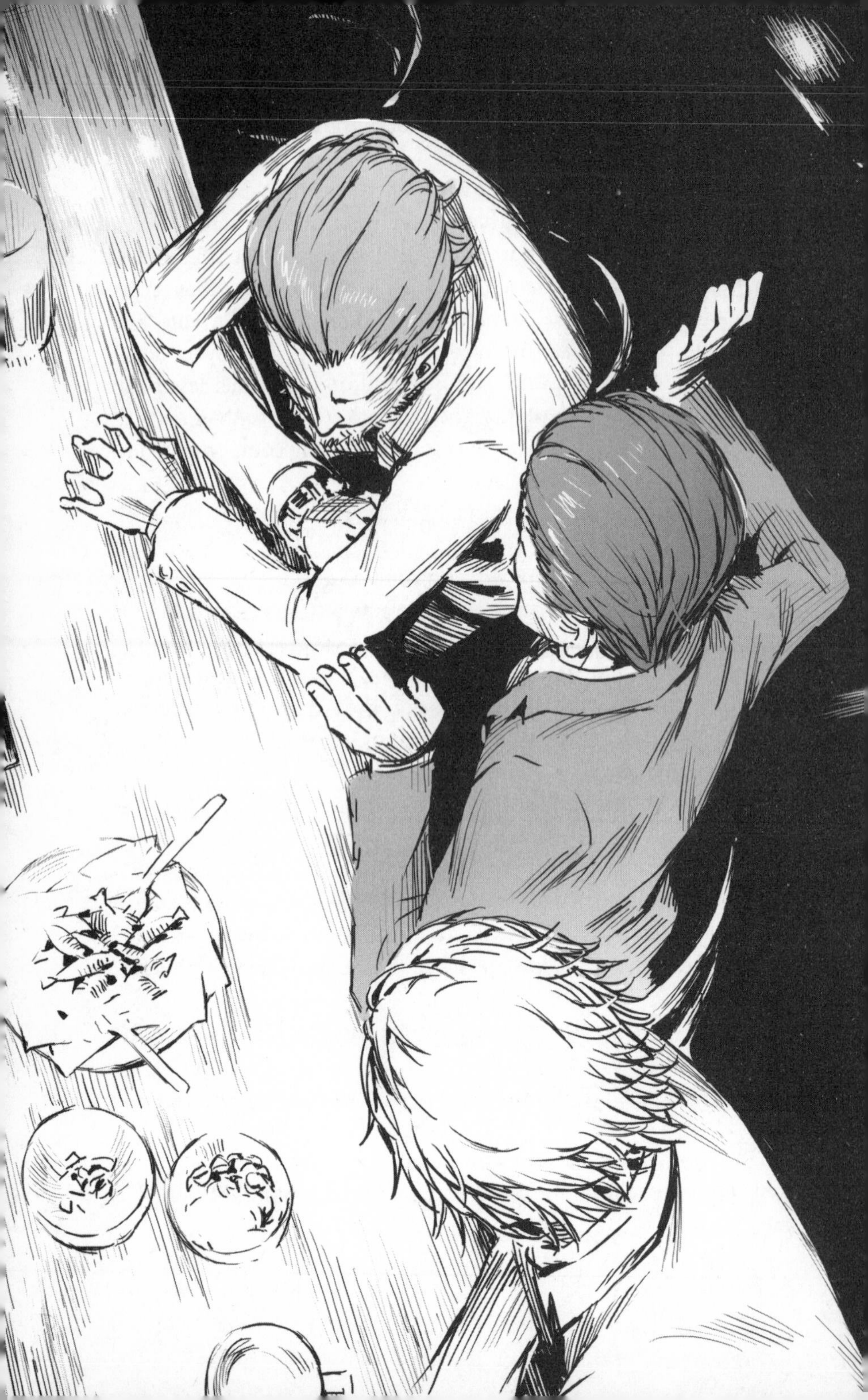

"?" Touya looked at Misaka dubiously. Misaka explained, his expression unamused:

"I mean, she seems t'be a prostitute."

Pfffrrrt!! Touya and Tanaka both sputtered loudly at the same time. Touya took a handkerchief out of his pocket, wiped off the weird sweat that had suddenly appeared on his face, and said, "W-wait, is that really all right? I don't think it is—like, legally speaking, and also it's absolutely shameful to say that about someone!"

"I mean, this isn't Japan, so…"

Come to think of it, he was right.

Tanaka then assumed a very gentlemanly look. After making up his mind—about something—he jumped to his feet.

"I've won."

"Won what?!"

"Heh-heh. Kamijou, as a married man, you're chained down right now! But I, a single man without a girlfriend, am different!! I have a one hundred percent chance of victory here!! Ha-ha-ha! This feels great! I'll get you back for all those times you showed off your young, beautiful wife!!"

So shouting, new employee Tanaka dashed over to the table in the back of the pub. The young woman glanced at the approaching Asian with suspicion. Without any introductions, much less a preface, he straight up asked, in English:

"How much for tonight?!"

A moment later, the blond-haired, blue-eyed, sexy lady, still sitting in her seat, made a fist and unleashed it on him. With a dull *wham*, her fist buried itself in Tanaka's crotch. In his current state, Tanaka likely keeled over and collapsed, but Touya and Misaka could only guess because they had both covered their eyes to avoid the sight of the aftermath. Tanaka eventually came back, crawling on the floor, unable to even walk.

And then he shouted, "She…she was just a regular office worker, you stupid drunk!!"

"Really? That's weird… I thought for sure she was a lady of the night," said Misaka lightheartedly, earning him a sharp glare from the woman. Apparently, she could understand their Japanese. Misaka downed his extra beer to cover up his surprise and continued, "And anyway, average corporate warriors like ourselves shouldn't be contemplating adventures like that."

"You think so?" said Tanaka.

"Hitting up a prostitute in some dingy pub in the corner of a fancy city like London?" said Touya. "Clearly fraught with danger, wouldn't you say? Even troublemaking main characters in comic books never try and cross *that* rope bridge."

"Oh, right. Either of you two know what an Uncut Gem is? It's like a different thing from Academy City…"

The inebriated Misaka started talking about something. Touya started ignoring him. "The important thing is not to stick your neck in any funny business like a *certain* troublemaker. Doing things you're not used to is bound to cause problems. If you do anyway, well—you end up getting wrapped up in trouble you'd never have been able to imagine normally… Just look at my son. Scares me so much I can't even laugh at it anymore."

"But still, if you want romantic encounters, I mean," stammered Tanaka, "if you're searching them out then, I mean, you've gotta be adventurous, right?"

"What I'm saying is that there's no need to gamble. You're still young. Go have an average encounter."

"What the heck is an *average encounter* anyway? Running into beautiful women is average for you at this point anyway—I mean, damn, would you *please* do something about that? It makes me want to punch you in the face!"

As Touya gave a great belly laugh, he suddenly felt someone tugging at his sleeve. "Hmm?" he said, looking that way to see a girl in her late teens who was dressed in oddly revealing clothing. She said nothing. She just stared into Touya's eyes.

"Who could that be?" asked Tanaka.

"It's the person we met yesterday, remember? Oh wait, you weren't there. She was wandering around near the station and I was wondering if she was lost, so I spoke up to…her…but…"

Touya's words trailed off.

He wasn't focusing on the girl's strangely alluring features, nor was he distracted by her curvy body, which was perfectly visible through the thin fabric. His eyes were on only the mysterious girl's right hand.

Something glittered on her slender wrist.

It was neither a wristwatch nor a bracelet.

Handcuffs.

And an attaché case that looked quite durable. The other handcuff was already hooked to its handle.

"Oh!"

Misaka, who had been left behind for a short time, pointing at it, said this as the kicker:

"How unusual. You're an Uncut Gem, aren't you?"

The strange, sudden term had a disquieting air about it.

Just as a bad premonition settled on Touya, the door to the pub crashed in with a *bang!!*

A group of unknown black-clothed people appeared in the doorway.

But they weren't even the most menacing thing in the room.

Greeahhh!!

With a crazy noise, it was the *girl* who mowed down the entire group of black-suits in one hit.

"You who have been caught in dangerous territory," said the girl in her late teens quietly, without turning around. "You seem to have become entangled in a troublesome issue, but you will be fine now. I give you my word that I will safeguard your life."

Touya Kamijou wasn't one to stick around and listen to every last word.

He disappeared out the back door in a flash. He was an international corporate warrior—one who had gone on business trips to war-torn South American countries armed with only a single management strategy. His survival instincts were *not* to be underestimated. The new employee Tanaka had followed suit and fled with him, quickly and wisely, and they began shouting curses at each other.

"Look, what the hell did I tell you?!" shouted Touya. "Average corporate warriors like us can't be biting off more than we can chew! We end up jumping into abnormal situations like this one!! That's why I said it was fraught with danger!!"

"But you're the one who brought the trouble to us in the end, Kamijou! I knew you were this kind of person right from the start! How much delicious trouble do you end up in wherever you go anyway?! Your wife is probably crying!!"

"I have a theory—that the girl was actually unrelated, and that office lady you talked to was actually the daughter of some shady organization's boss!"

"Depending on how the story progresses, that sounds like a rom-com waiting to happen, but look—that girl is right on our tail."

"Damn it! Now I'm *definitely* the source of all this!!"

He looked behind him and saw the strange handcuff-plus-attaché-case girl.

After getting tossed around by the stormy waves of ludicrous trouble, the corporate warriors, in the end, blew up a Cessna flying in the sky and pretended to be dead, but there is something that needs to be said regarding all that.

"It'll be fine!! If we put our heads together, we'll get through this, I'm positive!!"

"It's no good! I can't see any possible way to win!!"

"Hah! This has *nothing* on the things that crop up when I'm with my wife!!"

"It's no good! He started talking about his wife even at a time like this!!"

With a dash of this and that, the stimulating night in London pressed on.

CHAPTER 11

Every Field Has Its Exceptions
Second Friday of July

In a cafeteria that was supposed to be empty after lunch, a girl was taking a nap.

"Hey. Hey! You're attracting a lot of attention, you know."

That was a male teacher who had just happened to pass by the cafeteria. The girl, however—wearing a white short-sleeved sailor uniform—didn't answer him. She'd lined up three or four cafeteria chairs and was lying on top of them, lounging lazily.

When she realized the teacher wasn't leaving, she finally looked over at him, her eyes quite drowsy.

"...The beds in the nurse's office were the best, but they always chase me out of there."

"Are you trying to make a mockery of school life?"

"Not at all. To be clear, I love my current life."

"You do seem to be entertained, but the thing you're enjoying *isn't* school life. What grade are you anyway? And what class? I'm going to call your homeroom teacher—"

Before he could finish, though, his phone suddenly went off. Annoyed, the male teacher pushed the call button. As soon as he heard what the caller had to say, he immediately straightened up.

"Yes, yes, I'll be right there, sir," he said with all the respect in his tone he could muster before hanging up.

The girl, still looking sleepy, said in a bored way, "Seems pretty urgent."

"Damn it. I'm calling another teacher over. Right away."

The teacher exited the cafeteria with what sounded kind of like the mutterings of a sore loser.

"Don't run in the halls," said the girl. Unexpectedly, she actually got an angry shout in response. *He must be pretty wound up,* thought the girl offhandedly before checking to make sure nobody else was in the cafeteria. Then, still lying down, she reached for a device on the table.

The call had already started.

After giving a short yawn, the girl said into the device, "We should start soon, old-timer."

"Start what?"

"An unpleasant conversation."

The girl's name was Seria Kumokawa.

And the elder on the other end was Tsugutoshi Kaizumi.

"Seems like the outside world has been pretty noisy lately," she noted.

"As always, I must wonder where you get your information... You're referring to the Uncut Gems, yes?"

"You should be happy that I, your 'brain,' am so talented."

"That's the one catch you come with—how often you get off-topic like this..." Kaizumi breathed a sigh—the kind he'd never show his secretary or his subordinates—and prompted, *"What are you thinking?"*

"Leave 'em alone. They can't do anything."

"...What idiot would read those words in a report and be satisfied?"

"Sigh. You're such a plebe." Kumokawa poked her temple with an index finger a few times, still lying down. "Hypothetically, *could* you convince the real smart guys of Academy City to be satisfied with that? The twelve official General Board members, I mean. I find a good, cold glare stops most complaints."

"Government jobs aren't that easy, you know."

"If you're calling that post a *government job*, then you must be a real big shot," said Kumokawa, reaching for a convenience store bag on the table. It was packed with dessert-type sandwiches, with whipped cream and fruit. "Oh, well. I'll think about it a little more seriously, I guess."

"Don't talk with food in your mouth."

"About the Uncut Gems," continued Kumokawa, still lying down and now shoving a sandwich in her mouth, "it's true that we're late finishing the list. The U.S. and Russia probably caught on to how Academy City is making a list, too. They started making their own internal lists by themselves, and they're rejecting offers for cooperation. At this rate, it might affect our *work*."

"...And how does that link to you saying 'Leave them alone; they can't do anything'?"

"I'm not finished yet," said Kumokawa brusquely. "This time, I think our concern is how to efficiently *destroy* the issue of the Uncut Gems scattered around the world, don't you?"

"Indeed."

"And what you all were worried about, if I recall, is how other agencies might analyze the Uncut Gems and create supernatural Ability Development organizations that rival Academy City."

"Indeed."

"Then there's no problem. Let's see... The U.S. and Russia are the ones making moves at the moment, are they? Heh-heh. Still can't get rid of their dreams even after failing during the Cold War, eh? Unfortunately for them, their research won't get anywhere. No matter how many samples they have, they'll never understand what the data from them means."

"How can you say that for sure?" asked Kaizumi, a little bit of doubt creeping into his voice.

"Regarding the Russian laboratory. This so-called fully implemented psychic that a certain country created—the crystallization of their cutting-edge technology—apparently activates their unusual power by calling out to Mary and praying fervently... Well, I'm not about to reject other religions, and if that's how they focus their mind, then that's just how it is, but... Do you get what I'm trying to say? Why did they specifically choose to create a *scientific* research facility? They don't know what is mysterious, what isn't, and what kinds of mysterious things they're even looking for in the first place. They can't catch up to us by just lumping a bunch of people together."

"......"

"When it comes to human technology, eventually anyone will be able to catch up. But not if you can't even see the path you're supposed to be taking."

Seria Kumokawa's face looked quite unamused. Some of the drowsiness appeared to be gone, as though she'd just drunk some bitter tea that had roused her.

"Still not convinced?"

"Of course not. Your opinion has no evidence."

"Then you just need to gather some evidence yourself." Her tone was brusque as usual. "A bunch of self-proclaimed development organizations will pop up, but Uncut Gems are extremely rare in the world. There can only be around fifty total... And unlike those weird-ass scholars, they don't just pop up all the time. They're just irregulars without so much as a couple classes under their belt; barbarians struggling like insects. It's pretty clear which we should consider to be more important and treat as a priority, right?"

"So that is your conclusion after all..."

"I doubt such a move will be necessary, but we can't help it if you're not convinced. There will be more paperwork, and you'll just have to put up with it. As the brains of this operation, that's all I can say."

For a few moments, there was silence.

Eventually, Kaizumi said, *"What...exactly is an Uncut Gem?"*

"Yes, I'd expect that question from someone blinded by Academy City's science—like how you assume from the start that humans are the only ones who can create psychics and espers."

"Well, I understand them on a theoretical level."

Kaizumi seemed to be choosing his words carefully. But the fact that Kumokawa realized that meant he'd already failed. She'd been employed as the brains of the operation—he shouldn't have bothered trying to come off as smart.

"The ones Academy City makes are like artificial diamonds—and if the exact same environment occurs in the natural world, natural diamonds can occur, too... But I'm asking about something deeper. What are Uncut Gems?"

"......"

"There are several elements in Academy City that are noteworthy, too. Deep Blood, for example, and Imagine Breaker... I'm quite sure those are hardly normal abilities. They seem completely different in their direction than more easily categorized abilities like generating fire or electricity."

"Sounds like an idiot is worrying like an idiot would. Hmph," sniffed Kumokawa before answering. "It's just their special properties—including Academy City's Number Seven, who you seem so eager to pick apart. They're not strong, they're *rare*. In that sense, they're decently valuable for us as well."

They're only rare, though—the issue is that the percentage of espers with any practical use is pretty small, thought Kumokawa.

"And another thing. As the brains of the operation, I'll give you a piece of advice, since you're still *technically* a scholar."

"What?"

"I wouldn't categorize Imagine Breaker as a simple Uncut Gem." She paused. "I don't know the details, but it's probably...something much, *much* more interesting than whatever we think it is."

"......" Kaizumi fell silent for a moment. The brains had just said she *didn't know*. He was probably mulling that over. *"...You seem to find it fun,"* he finally said.

"Naturally. It's my job to think, after all."

Once homeroom was over, the stage moved to the school after hours. Mixed in with the flood of students going to their clubs or to hang out in the city walked a boy with spiky black hair.

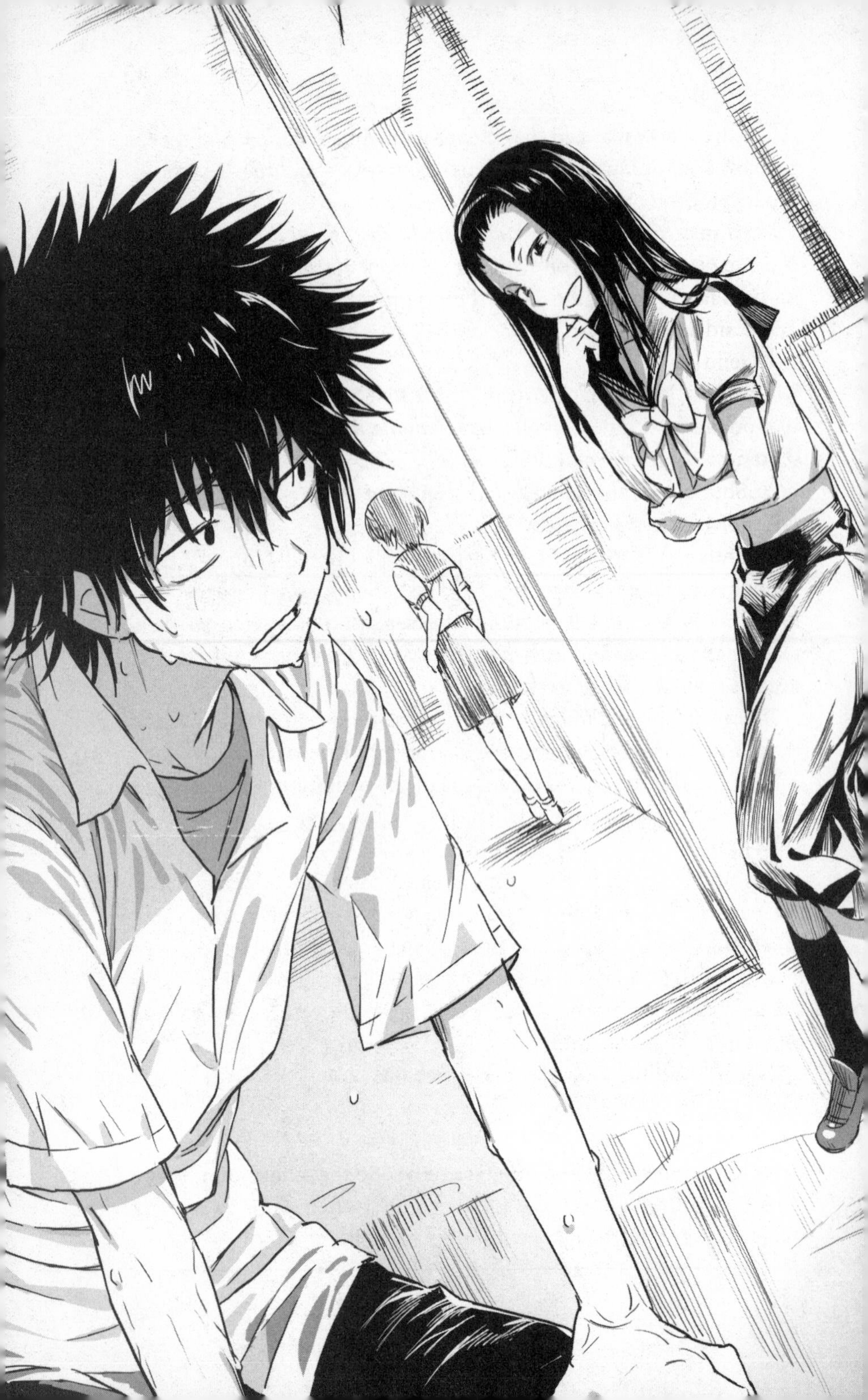

This boy, however, was a very unlucky one. Today, for no reason in particular, a sprinkler he happened to walk under randomly malfunctioned and started spraying directly at him, and only him. Bathed in a shower of water like a theater spotlight, the boy made a strange *bwahhh* noise.

A girl in a white, short-sleeved sailor uniform came over afterward.

She sidled up to the soaking-wet spiky-haired boy and, without even lending him a towel or a handkerchief, simply stood there and laughed.

"Looks like yet another incomprehensible thing has happened to you."

"…Shut up. Just my rotten luck again."

"I wonder how that rotten luck works anyway. You might discover some interesting rules or something if you looked into it in detail."

"Ugh. You're enjoying this, aren't you, Kumokawa?"

"Of course I am. I do so love my current life," she responded, laughing some more. Then she added, "After all, this school has so much in the way of entertainment."

CHAPTER 12

The Debate According to a Sniper and a Bomber
Fourth Friday of July

It happened three days ago.

When she'd told him, to his face, that snipers were old news.

"......"

Chimitsu Sunazara, who *did* sort of make a living as a hired sniper, could do nothing but keep his mouth shut. But as he cleaned the barrel of the last bit of soot, the woman kept on going.

"And doesn't sniping have a lot of unnecessary bits? Aiming for someone's head or chest, using five-millimeter bullets or seven millimeter or what have you—isn't that just a waste of time? I think it is. A little unaccounted wind and your bullet goes astray, too. Target sneezes, *bam*, mission failed. They wear bulletproof gear, you might not land a killing shot. It's all so *unnecessary*."

"......"

The woman was tall—even taller than Sunazara, who had a well-built physique. And she was *thin*. One might say she had the body of a model, and she *was* certainly beautiful, with pretty features to match. But that wasn't very compatible with this job—too much conspicuous beauty tended to be a liability when it came time to lie low.

Hiding didn't only mean wearing camo in the jungle and holding your breath, after all. For sniping jobs in large cities, for example, it was critical to blend in with the crowds while en route to a vantage point. And after the job, it was just as important to slip back into the crowds and leave quietly. *She*—Stephanie Gorgeouspalace—was not meant for such things.

Sunazara figured she should quit being an assassin and climb up onto a stage where she was supposed to be.

"Hmm? Sunazara, you're not sulking, are you?"

"…No, I am not," he replied idly. "But as someone in the same line of work, let me ask you. Could you do this job without sniping?" He gestured with his jaw at the map laid out on the table as he reassembled the cleanly wiped gun barrel. Before them was the layout of stereotypical villains and the bodyguards predictably surrounding them.

"These idiots engaged in supernatural ability fraud with the Kakyoukei Group," he said. "If I recall, they were raking in money from all over advertising that if someone would just pay them, they could get a supernatural Ability Development organization up and running that worked differently than Academy City. How would you plan to take this guy out?"

They weren't the type of group you could handle by just charging in with a knife, and they weren't stupid enough to let someone plant bombs on their vehicles. Sunazura thought the quickest way about it was to exploit the ten or so seconds it took them to go from exiting a building to climbing aboard their bulletproof cars to put a lead bullet right between the target's eyes…

"You have it all wrong. I'm not saying *everything* about sniping is anachronistic, okay? All I'm saying is that using a sniper rifle the way you do is old-fashioned. I wasn't trying to completely reject the utitity of sniping as a concept."

"……"

"You *are* sulking, aren't you?"

"I am not," said Sunazara as he put the dust cover on the exposed frame. This time he reached for the aiming mechanism.

As she watched Sunazara go about it, Stephanie said, "Just because you're going to snipe someone doesn't necessarily mean you have to use lead bullets, does it? We have all sorts of weapons in this day and age—wouldn't it be better to put them into your plans somehow?"

"What is it you're trying to say?"

"To be frank, wouldn't, like, a missile launcher or something be easier?"

"......"

"Whoa! Sunazara, you're making a face like I just committed a cardinal sin!! But really, though—wouldn't that be way simpler, though? When you're sniping, you'll fail if you miss a vital spot by even the tiniest of margins. But if you land a missile anywhere in the general area, they'll just blow up, and *boom*, target dead, right?! And it doesn't matter if they're wearing armor, either! It's gotta be way easier!!"

"...Hmph."

"Did you just snort at me?! You can only reach out to about a thousand meters with a rifle if you really tried, right? Couldn't you reliably hit targets five times that distance with a missile? Wouldn't it mean you could handle way more kinds of missions?!"

"Fine, then. It's your job. If you can do it with what you've procured yourself, all will be well."

"Don't need to tell me twice!!" said Stephanie, her breath wild as she took out a missile launcher that looked brand-new. It was the kind that fired from the shoulder, and she seemed to have chosen a surface-to-air launcher, rather than an anti-tank one... Even though she was attacking a ground target.

"Speaking of cardinal sins..."

"It'll be fine! As long as it kills the target!!"

That was the entire conversation they'd had three days ago.

Currently, Stephanie Gorgeouspalace was sobbing to herself in front of Chimitsu Sunazara.

"...You failed."

"No I didn't!"

"...News programs are calling it a miraculous survival against all odds."

"I'm telling you, I didn't fail!!" Stephanie jumped at Sunazara in an attempt to snatch the TV remote away from him. "I'm *sure* I blew him off the face of the Earth with that missile! Even his bodyguards got blown up!! And I made double sure they couldn't escape, either!! They must have hidden the corpses and the fact that the target died, and now they're reporting a cover-up!! Isn't that unfair? Now I'm not getting paid—isn't that a breach of contract?!"

"...This is why I told you not to use a messy method like missiles."

"You never said that! You never said anything like that to me even once!!"

Sunazara, dodging around Stephanie as she lunged at him, used the remote to change the channel. Every news station was basically reporting the same thing.

"Blowing them all up at once was your downfall. If you'd quickly presented them with a single corpse, they wouldn't have had any way to deceive everyone."

Sunazara sighed, tired.

"From your client's point of view, it didn't matter whether or not the target actually lived or died. Right now, the rest of society considers the guy to still be alive. That's why all our clients demands assassins have the skill to kill cleanly and with certainty."

"...Urp."

"Why else would we go to the trouble of infiltrating heavily guarded police parades to put a bullet right between the target's eyes in front of a huge audience? It's better to trade some damage for not letting them make excuses. Seeing a target's head blow up, especially, is the easiest to understand—that's why it's effective. The reason old-fashioned methods are still appreciated in modern times is because they're just that reliable. Unlike this utter foolishness."

Sunazara tossed the remote aside. He pushed away Stephanie, who was clinging close to him, and asked, "What are you going to do now?"

"Huh? What do you mean?"

"...You failed in a spectacular manner. In this situation, it's going to be extremely hard to rekill a target who is, from society's viewpoint, still alive. In a way, you've created an even worse situation than when the guy was alive. That's more than enough reason for your client to resent you now."

"Geh."

"Didn't you think this through? You're beyond foolish—you're an idiot."

As he watched Stephanie start to fidget and panic, Sunazara finally sighed. And then he grabbed the sniper rifle case from on the table.

"Let's go," he said.

"Huh? Are we going on the lam?!"

"Your client was the Kakyoukei Group—national borders don't matter to them. If you want to survive, you'll just have to rekill the target."

"?" Stephanie angled her head.

Sunazara poked his jaw toward the TV screen. "I'd initially thought this was something a journalist drafted as a cover, but it's too believable, considering what we know about the target... I can only assume he's alive after all."

"Huh? But..."

"Did you witness the exact moment the target exploded? And if it had, it might have been a body double. In any case, he probably took advantage of all this chaos to convince others in the under-world that he'd died, and now he's likely trying to prevent any follow-ups."

"Umm... Does that mean...there's still a chance?"

"Yes," answered Sunazara. "Good thing, too. Your incredibly shoddy, inexperienced skills have given you an opportunity to make it out alive. Assassins who can't provide evidence of their kills are even lower than housewives angrily swinging around ashtrays under assumptions of cheating. If it were me, I'd never die from explosives, no matter what the situation."

"Woooow!! Sunazara, you're being unusually scathing today!!"

Of course I am, he thought bitterly.

After all, he had to help clean up after the mess this idiot caused by blowing her shot. And *this* sniping job would be *pro bono*.

CHAPTER 13

The Precision of Group Fortune-Telling

Fourth Friday of August

About ten girls, all with the exact same face, had been admitted to a certain hospital in School District 7 of Academy City. They were the Sisters—military-use clones made with a certain Level Five esper's somatic cells. Drugs and various techniques had forcibly accelerated their growth, shortening their life spans as a result. To overcome that, one doctor of questionable repute had been personally making "adjustments" to them here and there.

As for their actual appearance, they had fair skin, brown eyes, and brown hair, and they wore Tokiwadai Middle School's summer uniform, consisting of an ash-colored pleated skirt, a white blouse, and a beige summer sweater. Nothing necessitated that they all wear the same clothing just because they were clones, but that was how they all were now, whether it was because of the effects of the brain wave network linking their minds together or their personalities having all been leveled out during the clone creation process.

Right now, they were in what the hospital called the Clinical Research Area. It wasn't exactly cordoned off, but it was located in an odd place, built quite far from the route connecting the main hospital building and other necessary facilities so that nobody would wander into it by chance.

Four Misakas—numbers 10032, 10039, 13577, and 19090—were standing there idly in the small waiting room set up in a corner of the Clinical Research Area's hallway. The only things here were a perfunctory sofa and table, a few magazines meant purely for passing the time, and a rack for those magazines thrown in for good measure. The four clone girls, having plucked one issue from the stack, had it open to a certain page, which they were staring at veeeeeeeeeeeeeeeeeeeeeery carefully.

It was the horoscope section.

Far from the genuine (?) occult fortune-telling, this was the kind of column that could be found in every magazine; they were always buried in the pages somewhere, as common as pickled ginger paired with sushi. The page was separated into twelve sections, each giving a simple overview for each sign regarding general things, like what would bring fortune or misfortune, health, or luck with money or romance, plus a lucky color and a lucky item.

"If we convert Misaka's production date into Greek zodiac format, it would give…"

Number 10032—also called "Little Misaka" by a certain spiky-haired boy—focused on her own fortune.

This month you'll have an AMAZING chance to change up your job! If you've ever wanted to say good-bye to that awful boss you see on a daily basis, now's the time!!

"……"

Job changes meant literally nothing to a mass-production clone made for military purposes. Number 10032 cocked her head slightly.

The other Sisters seemed to have generally similar reactions as they each read the horoscope section corresponding to their manufacturing date, with some of them tracing the text with their fingers.

"Can the Misakas truly gain benefit from such uncertain information? says Misaka number 10039, giving voice to her question."

"In what way, exactly, will this 'lucky item' bring fortune to Misaka? I wonder, says Misaka number 13577, deciding for now to search for a keychain with a cat on it anyway."

"Th-this month's luck in romance is minus five—but that's impossible, says Misaka number 19090, requesting a do-over."

Number 19090 spoke in an oddly mumbling voice for some reason, but the other girls weren't about to worry over such a thing. Number 10032 suddenly brought her face up, as though she'd just realized something.

"...Before anything else, when should we consider our birth to have occurred? says Misaka number 10032, conducting a reaffirmation of fundamental definition settings."

"?"

"It is true that our manufacturing dates are tied to the exact time we were removed from our cultivators, but not all ten thousand Misakas were pulled from these containers at exactly the same time—we were shipped after we had matured to the physical age of fourteen via drugs and other such things, says Misaka number 10032, adding a long-winded supplementary explanation."

"Which would make our birth similar to a daughter who grew to fourteen years old in her mother's womb, in human terms, before actually exiting, says Misaka number 10039, deciding to go along with what the Misaka next to her is saying."

"...Well, can't we just assume that the exact time that we came out of our mother's womb is also our time of birth, regardless of how much we matured beforehand? says Misaka number 13577, transmitting a differing opinion."

"No, we Misakas must have been inside several different machines depending on our development stages, so how would we classify such cases? says Misaka number 19090, as her mind fills with question marks."

The Sisters continued to mutter, mumble, and whisper their conversation.

"Or perhaps the date we should commemorate for our emergence should be the day approval was granted for the production project planned based on all Misakas' DNA mapping, says Misaka number 10032, offering a different idea."

"In human terms, would that not correspond to the date our father and mother engaged in intercourse? argues Misaka number 10039."

"Actually, would that not correspond to the date the sperm was created inside the father's body prior to intercourse? says Misaka, tracing back in time."

"*Pfft*, says Misaka number 19090, deciding for now to make her astonishment at the recent trend in the conversation clear."

The Sisters were even equipped to process witty retort functions by themselves.

Then, Misaka number 10032 rubbed her temples with her fingers. "...Actually, the project to manufacture us Misakas was split into two steps: the Radio Noise project and the Level Six Shift project, if I recall correctly, says Misaka number 10032, making the matter even more tangled up in her mind. Which project should we even refer to the acceptance date of?"

"Oh, well—is it not true that it is always preferable to refer to the earlier? says Misaka number 10039, offering her own predictive information in a vague manner."

"Strictly speaking, because these two projects possess different characteristics—the former in its aim for a perfected Level Five and the latter in its demand to mass-produce experimental subjects—it may be rather difficult to determine definitions for this matter, says Misaka number 13577, quietly spurring confusion where none was asked for."

"Come to think of it, I wonder where Ao Amai's number 00000, Full Tuning, who was severed from the network, is right now and what she is doing, says Misaka number 19090, introducing a new piece of foreshadowing."

After finally throwing their hands up in the air, concluding that horoscopes made no sense, they settled on a forward-looking perspective that they would carve out destinies for themselves with their own hands.

"...But then Misaka found this, says Misaka number 10032, presenting even further kindling for the fire."

""""?"""""

The other three girls turned to her and saw that in number 10032's hands was a different magazine from the one they'd been using.

Flipped to a page near the back, it had a certain column in it, with even less space on the page granted to it than the horoscopes.

It was blood-type fortune-telling.

"...What could they be up to?" said a baffled young nurse who had been observing the four girls from a short distance away.

Next to her, a frog-faced doctor, after sipping some coffee from a paper cup, said, "It looks like they're having an argument, hmm?"

"Well, yes, but that isn't what I meant. Actually, I'll just say it again. What *are* they doing?"

Even as their exchange continued, the four girls with the exact same face continued their own discussion.

"What! The luck in romance for type AB is exceptional! reports Misaka number 10032!!"

"If you're going to say that, then Misaka, being type AB, is exceptional as well! reports Misaka number 10039!"

"No! This Misaka, as a *super*-type AB above all other Misakas, is *super*-exceptional! says Misaka super-number 13577, snatching victory for herself!!"

"No, no, the one who will have the last laugh is *this* Misaka, says Misaka number 19090, declaring her hegemony over the AB world!!"

Hair was being pulled, clothes were being yanked, magazines were being stolen, panties were being exposed—it was a chaotic free-for-all.

The young nurse's face was one of blank amazement. "Those girls—they convert brain waves into electronic signals to form one giant network, right?"

"Ah, you're referring to the Misaka network?"

"Wouldn't that also mean that while they each have their own identities, because the giant network itself functions as one large brain, each of them is under interference from a single overarching will?"

"Yes, I suppose you could put it like that, hmm?"

"...Then how are they having an *argument*?"

That was what the young nurse seemed incapable of grasping.

The frog-faced doctor stuck out his tongue—the coffee was a little too bitter for him. "Regular people are always picking one action from several choices. For example, when dieting, they might have two thoughts at the same time when presented with a slice of cake: that they want to eat it even if they put on weight and that they *don't* want to eat it *because* they'll put on weight."

"Um, right."

"Well, regular people just have to whittle down the options in their head one by one, then output the final remaining choice as their action. We only have one body, so even if we have multiple viewpoints, we still have to commit to a single action in reality, hmm?"

"Then you're saying it's...?"

"Yes. In their case, since one overarching will is influencing multiple physical bodies, there's no need for them to converge on a single thought process. For them, *everything* is valid. Eating the cake despite getting fat and not eating it because you'll get fat—they don't have to pick just one. They can choose both. They have multiple bodies to act on it, right?"

"......"

The young nurse looked again at the girls, whose panties were now fully exposed. Could she currently be witnessing an incredibly valuable sight?

"As a result, the same influence on the girls from the one overarching will is only going in one direction—each of the specimens is beginning to acquire distinct behavioral tendencies. That's why they can have conversations with other Misakas and fight with them. Isn't that a good thing? From a human perspective?"

The frog-faced doctor didn't seem to mind it very much.

As he ran his fingers down the paper cup with the bitter coffee in it, he said the next thing in a way that could have been taken as neglectful.

"Let's just pray that they eventually mature into full-fledged individuals."

CHAPTER 14

Dances of Gatekeepers and Intruders
Third Friday of September

To restate something mentioned previously, Kazari Uiharu was *not* superhuman.

"?"

As she was munching on a cookie after school in the offices of Judgment Branch 177, she glanced at the laptop on her steel desk as though she'd just noticed something.

Mrfh?! A bother has arrived!!

An intruder.

Not one worming into Uiharu's computer or one breaking into Judgment Branch 177. Uiharu had been tasked with countering the recent string of electronic attacks on the data banks, which managed all the information networks in Academy City. As part of the new security measures, changes had been made to direct all data requests to route through a large Judgment server first, forcing them to take a roundabout path.

Now, some data was ignoring the detour and making a beeline for the data banks.

The flow of the data was absolutely impossible via normal control.

It was clearly a hacking attempt.

And it wasn't any regular hacking attempt. It wasn't, for example, trying to take advantage of security holes to go through unintended routes and gain access. Uiharu had already closed up any silly holes.

Which meant…

A young lady from Tokiwadai Middle School, famed for its esper Ability Development, sat on a bench at a station. She was none other than Mikoto Misaka. The tablet in her hands was currently connected to the network via wireless LAN.

She was one of only seven Level Five espers in Academy City.

The Railgun.

She was ranked third in all the city but first among her peers when it came to manipulating electricity.

Though she was directly touching the screen with her index finger to control it, the actions playing out on the display were undoubtedly happening much faster and in much larger quantities than her finger movement would suggest. Rows of symbols and characters scrolled by so fast it was hard to follow them with the eye; Mikoto wasn't paying attention to every single one. All she was doing was transferring the ideas in her head into the machine—the computer took it upon itself to do the work, almost like it was simply a natural consequence of her thinking it.

Mikoto was trying to access Academy City's data banks.

She'd infiltrated them several times in the past, but she'd yet to be stopped by anyone higher up the ladder. It seemed they, to their credit, had suspicions they may have *possibly* been hacked, but it had never resulted in her suddenly being cut off from the network entirely and blocked.

…Well, that's a rough decision for them to have to make anyway. Everything would suffer, right down to the timing of trains having to make emergency stops.

Blip-blip-blip-blip-blip-blip-blip-blip-blip. As she looked at the windows appearing and disappearing, one after the next, she sighed quietly.

She wanted to use her full power to get this over with already, but she didn't want to do anything that would wreck her own device, either.

*　　*　　*

...Hmm. Uiharu returned the half-eaten cookie to the plate as she watched the intrusion trying to directly access the data banks. *This kind of thing happened before, too. It looks a little more advanced than last time, though.*

As she looked at the information on the screen, she sighed.

What was happening before her eyes was a phenomenon that was absolutely impossible with regular computer usage.

Which meant the hacker was using an ability.

Academy City was a city of espers. Plenty of them could do things like this, of course. Some could read minds to steal passwords; others could manipulate electrons to gain control over computers; and worst of all, there were even some who could directly manipulate the data itself.

It was nigh impossible to take down hackers like that through normal tech-based countermeasures alone. The difference between the average user and hackers simply came down to how much of the system's interface they could access, and how much they could ferret out from behind the curtains. However, people relying on their ability for access were basically going one layer deeper than everyone else.

Of course...

This was Academy City—a city brimming with espers.

I can't protect peace and order if I let something like this scare me off!!

Renewing her resolve, Uiharu checked the flow of data one more time. If they weren't using the "shortest route" that Uiharu had set up ahead of time, then they weren't reading her thoughts. The spike of data wasn't slipping through the barriers themselves or ignoring them completely, so it seemed likely the system itself wasn't being directly manipulated.

Which means...

This was probably the type of esper who could control electrons. And since that was a relatively common esper variety, it was pretty much impossible to narrow down who the suspect might be with just this information.

"……"

Uiharu's brow furrowed as her eyes followed the intrusion's movement patterns.

With that tiny bit of data as a point of reference, she conceptualized the system as a flower.

What Uiharu was looking at now was the tip of its roots. From there, she would mentally map out things like the stem, the petals, the flow of water and nutrients—and eventually, she assembled the image of a complete flower in her mind. This method of calculation—envisioning a single mechanism from a variety of angles—was the key to Uiharu's hacking prowess.

If she had been especially talented, her mind might have constructed a staggeringly formidable personal reality and manifested it in the form of incredible power.

However…

…*Urgh*… Uiharu chewed on her lip.

Her mental image, which had started with the tips of the roots, suddenly blew apart once it reached around the stem. Her opponent must be using a very advanced method of calculation—she couldn't draw the connection between what was happening before her eyes and the personal reality that was causing it to happen.

And if she didn't understand her opponent, she couldn't devise a proper countermeasure.

What should I do…?

For a moment, Uiharu's fingers wandered in front of the keyboard.

The movement was like holding chopsticks aloft, but not knowing what food to reach for—and it perfectly symbolized her distress.

"All right, here we go," murmured Mikoto as she watched the swift developments flash by on the screen.

Currently, she was performing a typical password break.

Just because she was an esper who could control electricity didn't mean she could rely on that power alone to break through *every* security system. In fact, given how many espers resided in Academy City, the development of barriers against irregular attacks like that was actively being honed all the time.

But no matter how it was reasoned or rationalized, someone with an ability would always have the advantage over someone without one.

Of course, she wasn't going to use her ability alone to concentrate on a single point and bust through that way.

She didn't have to stubbornly cling to one method, after all.

She could take advantage of her electricity control to overcome difficult-to-unlock security on normal computers and use a normal computer to deal with security systems specialized to act against espers. By using both options efficiently, Mikoto was more than able to infiltrate various targets.

It didn't take long before her work ended without issue.

Mikoto tapped a few more keys, which brought her past the final line of security.

Now, then. Where could the data I'm looking for be hiding...hmm?

And then she froze.

She stared at the screen—her eyebrow was the only thing that twitched.

What she saw displayed there was...

...clusters of data from the data banks all being encrypted at an insanely fast pace.

No way...

As far as she could tell from the rows of characters switching randomly over to sequences of symbols and numbers, this was most likely Omega Secret being deployed to the Academy City network: that incredibly singular random-number encryption that had received the highest accolades from a certain little Absolute Encryption Contest.

No way, no way, no way!

The Absolute Encryption Contest was a major competition with no material prize, pitting humans and computers in the highest form of chess matches. But for all that, it was also famous for getting conspicuously sharp results. Omega Secret had been born there and it was famous for being unbreakable: After all, with the data encrypted randomly, even the programmers themselves couldn't read the perfectly protected data. It was a beast, the most advanced system available, with no actual practical use; it was said even Academy City supercomputers would take two hundred years to decrypt something like that.

What kind of complete idiot would bring out something like this?!

The troubling point about Omega Secret was that once something was encrypted, it didn't matter how small or how big a file was: They'd all take equal time, two hundred years, to decrypt. And since it used different random processing on every single file, a a single decryption key couldn't be applied to all of them even if one had been cracked. It would still take two hundred years to decrypt the next file.

The entirety of the data banks was being encrypted, and the contents were impossibly numerous, so Mikoto didn't know where the data she was after would be. She couldn't pick some to steal; the only method that was sure to get her the data she wanted would be for her to prepare an entirely new super-large-scale data bank equal to the data banks' storage server and literally copy everything over, but…

Well, she definitely couldn't do anything about *this*.

Even acquiring such a large server alone was practically impossible. If she somehow managed it, how long would it take to copy all the data in the data banks over to it? Despite their lenience in the past, those monitoring the situation were *not* about to ignore such a massive data exchange.

However…

…This is insane. They're encrypting everything—right down to the data banks' server management and deleted maintenance files!! Wouldn't that render their OWN high-capacity server totally useless?!

The cost of machines that used the data banks was so high that even Mikoto, a seasoned, upper-class young lady, would pale at the sight of the price tag. And they'd just thrown it all away without a second thought. It made her wonder if opening up the physical server and throwing a bucketful of water over it might have done *less* damage.

If their counterattack was this crazy, they must have a backup of the data banks' stored somewhere else. If I can attack that, I might be able to get the data I want, but...

Mikoto looked at the catastrophe on her screen again.

She got the feeling that her opponent was operating under zero limitations. She couldn't help but think that even if it was the very last copy of the data, they'd mercilessly use this method again if it meant bringing Mikoto down.

Hackers operate best undiscovered.

After hesitating for a few moments, Mikoto finally mussed her hair in resignation.

...I'll go by the book and withdraw for now. A desperate fight with this massive idiot would destroy us both. Makes me shudder.

"Well, I suppose that does it for today," murmured Kazari Uiharu as she watched her screen.

If the intruder had stuck around a little longer, she might have been able to try a reverse trace, but she'd accomplished plenty already this battle. Rather than chasing too doggedly, she'd be better off analyzing the hacker's attack patterns and using what she learned to prepare the data banks' defenses.

One might wonder if such normal methods would have any effect against a hacker who could control electricity, but of course they would. The opponent was still only taking advantage of a back door—their ability. It only *looked* like they were all-powerful because they were freely using that exception to travel about.

In concrete terms, they were doing nothing more than sending and receiving electronic signals. Because of the nature of that interaction, she could search out where that exception was happening and plug the hole, thus blocking an esper hacker with normal methods.

Well, everything's a new experience to be studied. That was a pretty good display of skill, so hopefully this ends up benefiting me, too.

And then it happened, just as Uiharu was thinking about this and reaching for the cookie on the plate.

"...Uiharu," came a low voice.

She turned around and saw Kuroko Shirai, her Judgment colleague, standing in the doorway. She was looking down at the ground. Uiharu tilted her head in confusion. Her twin-tailed job friend jabbed her thumb, pointing out the door, and said in an even lower voice:

"You went too far. And now they're going to lecture us, you moron."

CHAPTER 15
Art Separates the Geniuses from the Eccentrics
First Friday of October

A crowd of English Puritan Church combat personnel had gathered in a women's dorm in London. A woman with long black hair in a ponytail named Kaori Kanzaki was one of their number.

Normally, she carried a very long Japanese katana—over two meters long—called the Seven Heavens Sword at her waist.

The sheath is a wonderful decorative accessory for the sword. Would you not like to decorate your own beloved blade to be more beautiful?

There she stood by herself in the cafeteria, trembling, a flyer in her hands with *that* written on it.

On the pretty, four-colored flyer were several sample photos, each bordered by little squares, making the whole thing look like an open bento box seen from above; vermilion maple leaves on black ground and detailed gold-leaf animal cutouts adorned the other sections.

There was an audible gulp.

Kanzaki didn't realize she was the source of that sound.

Hrrrnnng…!! What is this?! I was just starting to think my cold, black sheath wasn't quite up to par. If I could get it decorated with these scarlet maple leaves or yellow cranes… N-no, no!! The true way of the Amakusa-Style Crossist Church is to extract and apply magical symbols from everyday items! I cannot recombine my sheath's symbols so easily... B-but... Perhaps these nighttime cherry blossom petals would not cause any iconographic issues...

Kaori Kanzaki, ordinarily the spitting image of a stereotypical cool and collected, traditional Japanese woman, kept groaning under her breath as she agonized over her choices. And then, as though to deliver the killing stroke, a different flyer slipped out of her hand and floated down to the cafeteria table.

On it was written this:

A suit of armor is the best partner you can have—it will always watch your back. We want you to feel the breath of this wonderful ally on your skin as it sits snugly wrapped around you even in the most precarious of situations.

"H-hrrrrnnnnnnnnnnnnnnnnnnnnnggg!!"

Staring a hole through the advertisement photos, which showed things that looked like dolls for the Boys' Festival in May, she thought, she couldn't possibly get a *complete* suit of armor, but perhaps just something for the arms and legs and a breastplate. Something she could integrate with her normal clothing— *No, no!!* she told herself, her mind racked with worries over this and that.

And then she came to her senses.

Her head snapped up, and as she quietly cleared her throat, she deliberately slid the flyers to the side. This wasn't the time to let herself be charmed by these flyers, left here as though someone had planned on laying a trap.

Kanzaki passed from the cafeteria into the kitchen space.

The clergy here had secured a considerably large area so they could prepare food for many people at once. There was an industrial oven, an industrial refrigerator, an industrial sink—every last thing in this kitchen had the word *industrial* attached, and upon entering it and popping open the huge silver refrigerator, Kanzaki removed a small storage container from its recesses.

The bony parts of an already-filleted sea bream.

Kanzaki was on cooking duty today, and she'd conserved the fish bones between meals. These parts she'd gotten from using a knife to whittle off the little pieces of flesh stuck to the thicker bones.

It had put her in a slight depression when a short-statured sister named Angeline, the one who always came by to snatch food away, had said something along the lines of *Wow, you have a really gluttonous appetite, huh,* but right now, Kanzaki could say it openly—that Sister Angeline was correct. Kanzaki had one specific favorite food.

Kanzaki took what was left of the rice in the giant rice cooker—the sort one might use for catering—and put it in a bowl before taking a pinch of the sea bream dregs and sticking them in the center. Then, after rapidly boiling the bream's bone and head, she stuck the resulting dashi broth in a teapot, then finally poured it over her rice bowl.

Gently, she put down the teapot, then brought her hands together in a soft clap that didn't create any noise.

"Heh-heh. Heh-heh-heh… Sea bream *chazuke*! ☆"

Wow, clap-clap-clap. There Kanzaki was, getting quietly excited by herself. It wasn't tea she was adding to the rice, so it wasn't technically *chazuke*—but it was still acceptable. Kaori Kanzaki liked the dashi broth variety better anyway. No matter what anyone else said, she swore she could eat this one dish for the rest of her life, even if she couldn't have anything else.

With this and that, Kanzaki felt it would take too long to bring her bowl into the cafeteria, so she took a pair of chopsticks from the cupboard and, already wiggling around her behind in her indigo-dyed yukata, wearing a smile, doing none of the above with any sort of consistent rhythm, she said:

"Okay. Time to dig i—"

"Who's eating something so delicious in the middle of the night?! Show yourself!!"

"It smells *so* good!! I'm too hungry to sleep right now after all!!"

Suddenly hearing several female voices cry out from the direction of the ceiling, followed by the pattering of footsteps, Kanzaki panicked. As she did, the frantic footfalls accelerated and multiplied, steadily making their way to her location.

She only had one sea bream *chazuke*.

It didn't matter if they'd sniffed it out—she couldn't acquiesce to their request.

Which meant there was only one thing to do.

At this rate, we'll have a mad scramble on our hands…!

Kanzaki steeled herself, snatched up the bowl with hot steam billowing from it, put her lips to the edge of it, and then began madly driving her chopsticks back and forth and slurping it down. She felt tears rising to her eyes, but she didn't have time to worry about it. This was the only way to stop the senseless conflict. It was *not*, of course, because she was afraid of others falling in love with the sea bream *chazuke* at first sight.

With the bowl empty, she threw her chopsticks into the dishpan, which was already filled with water, then washed down the scant remainder of the dashi broth left in the pan and the teapot. As the finishing touch, she sprayed some deodorizer everywhere.

Pshhh-pshh-pshh!!

All of it took her just thirty seconds.

Kanzaki returned the deodorizing spray to its original location and bolted upright just as she heard the *crash* of the door as a group of sisters overwhelmed with hunger came scampering into the kitchen.

Leading the charge was, as she'd expected, the short sister with blond hair in French braids, Angeline. Her little nose perked up as she sniffed around.

"K-Kanzaki! Did you see any mysterious people holding extremely delicious-looking food around here?!"

"N-no. You mean like a mysterious old man coming to deliver ramen or something? Not at all."

"That's strange. I could have sworn the smell was coming from this direction…"

Making a series of audible sniffing noises, Angeline wandered about the kitchen like a military hound who'd lost its prey. Behind her there were several other sisters following suit. Kanzaki slowly looked away from the group, casually glanced at the window, noticed in her reflection that a grain of rice was stuck to her lip, and hastily brushed it into her mouth.

In the meantime, the tall, cat-eyed Sister Lucia, who was always with Angeline and was here now, possibly having noticed all the ruckus, began talking to Angeline about something.

"Sister Angeline… What is the meaning of this?"

"It's autumn! And everyone knows autumn is for art! And I'm expressing myself through art."

Confused, Kanzaki looked over and saw Angeline had a chocolate coronet pastry in her hand, with three silver forks stuck into each side of the bread for a total of six. Seeing that, Lucia's eyes said it all: *How dare you play with your food; that's one hundred spanks for you.*

Holding the sweetbread, forks unfurling from it like some kind of wings, Angeline said, "This symbolizes the anger swirling inside me."

"Uh-huh."

"My heart is about to burst from my chest, full of rage and wrath. But it needs *energy* to burst out. And the exchange of that energy means that the anger I direct toward others will eventually come back to me—anyway, what I'm trying to say is, I'm so angry that it's made me even more hungry!!!!!!"

"……" Lucia sighed heavily. Now that Miss Angeline's audio commentary was over, it was time for those hundred spanks.

But just as she thought that, Sherry Cromwell, a sorcerer with blond hair like a lion, brown skin, and gothic-lolita-style clothing, came into the kitchen, having been later than the rest.

"It *is* art…!!"

"D-don't make jokes that are just going to fly over everyone's head!!" cried Lucia. "Look—now that you said that strange thing, Sister Angeline is gasping and having a peculiar flash of enlightenment!!"

What *seemed* like enlightenment was actually the result of Lucia

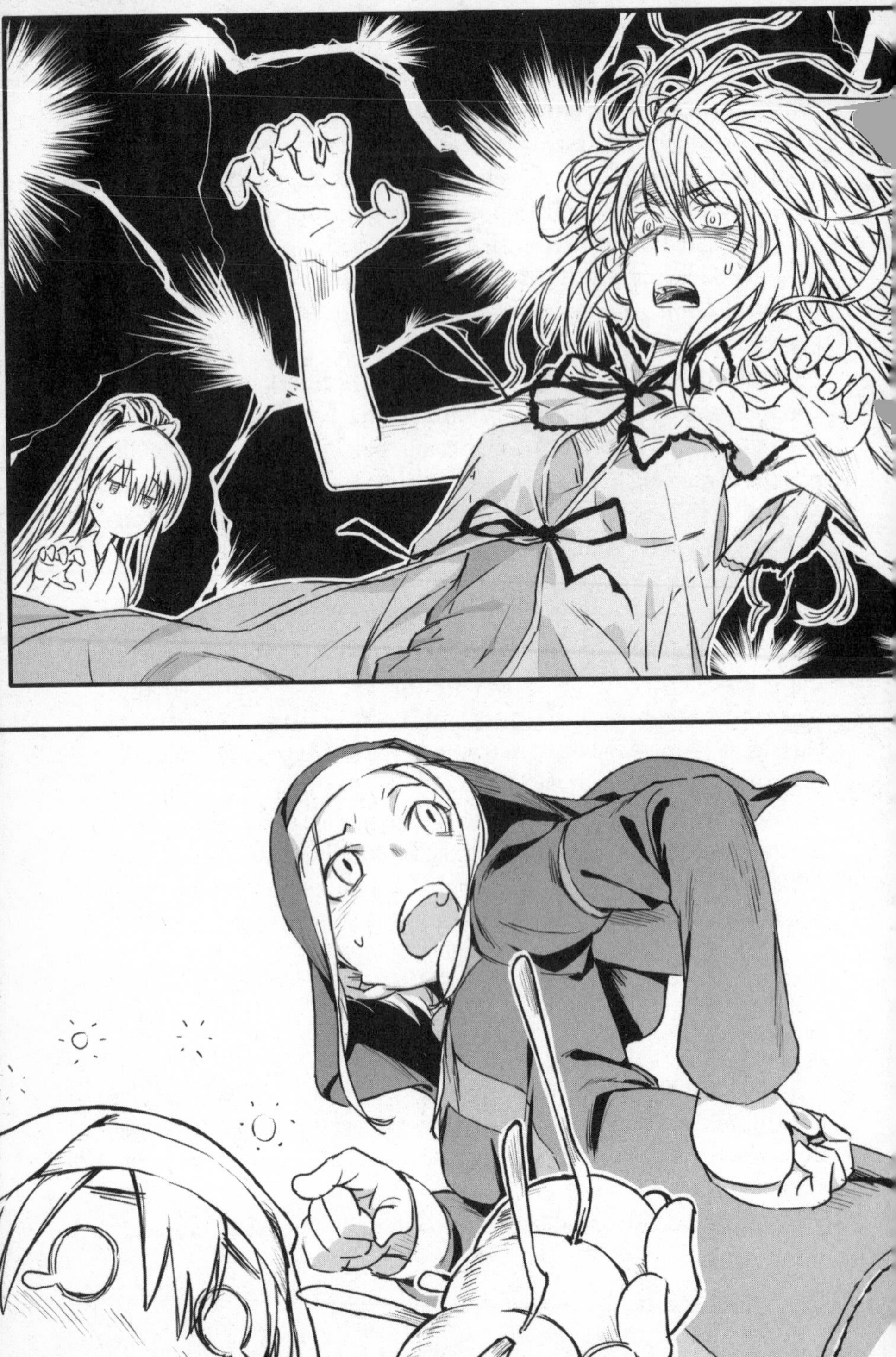

flaring up at Sherry, which caused Lucia to spank Angeline with 80 percent more power, but she didn't notice that fact.

Meanwhile, Sherry, for her part, as though showing respect to the sweetbread forks mysteriously invoking human emotions, put on thin gloves like she was about to handle a precious antique and said, "Hey! You two—the tall and short duo!!"

""Please don't refer to us like we're plumbers!!""

"…Can…can I touch that sw-sweetbread…? Wait!! I understand! I'm fully aware that I'm making a tactless request!! But since it's three-dimensional…I can't help but want to view it from all different angles…!!"

The dark-skinned sculptor seemed to be agonizing over something, but Lucia figured that it didn't matter to her if she was going to eat it. It quickly changed hands, but then Sherry started groaning and muttering. "The forks' directions… The shape of these wings… I see—so this symbolizes anger on an empty stomach making one even hungrier…!!"

The rest of the sisters began to file out of the kitchen, muttering that they simply didn't understand artists. Kanzaki slipped into their ranks, sighing. She'd gotten down the hallway when something suddenly struck her as strange.

Wait.

How did we get on the topic of art anyway?

CHAPTER 16

There's a Reason She Doesn't Look Like a Mother

First Friday of October

A membership sports gym, a short distance away from the hottest place in all Kanagawa Prefecture.

In a room where both the walls and ceilings were made of glass panes, the gym's indoor pool looked like the typical rectangle found in high schools, albeit classier and more intricate. The clientele was fairly varied; ranging from athletes trying to shave 0.1 seconds off their time to fitness seekers to housewives taking swim lessons.

Misuzu Misaka was swimming in one of the lanes on the edge of the pool.

She looked like she was squarely in her twenties, but she was actually a mother with a fourteen-year-old daughter. Every day, after her university lectures ended, she swam in this pool. It was exercise at least—for the subtle reason that if she let down her guard, it would come back to bite her—but her pace was remarkably quick. Though a female athlete in the next lane over had gotten herself fired up like a rival and was desperately trying to keep up, she didn't stand a chance with Misuzu slicing through the water with the force of a torpedo.

According to Misuzu, however...

...*This sucks.*

She pressed her hands against the edge of the pool, and then her face broke the water with a splash. Ignoring the instructors and others, who were speechless at the new speed record, she sighed, somewhat annoyed.

This swimsuit is so efficient there's no point in using it. I'm exercising in the water because it has a lot of resistance, but I think the swimsuit isn't helping...

Misuzu wasn't wearing a swimsuit, really, so much as a black wet suit–type thing, the kind surfers liked to wear. The suit's sleeves and legs were cleanly cut at the elbows and knees, and it emphasized her body much in the same way a one-piece would.

Anyway, she'd seen an advertisement saying it would let her swim faster, so she'd ordered it through the mail on a whim. Unfortunately, it was adjusting the water currents *too* efficiently. It would have been a grand success if she were competing in earnest, but it seemed the swimsuit wasn't designed with gym goers like her in mind.

And then...

"Oh, why, hello. Are classes over?" came a voice from the poolside.

"Mrs. Kamijou? Hello!" answered Misuzu, leaning back against the course rope and waving from the water.

Mrs. Kamijou was a woman named Shiina Kamijou. It seemed she'd moved here recently and had become a bit of a celebrity in the neighborhood as the "Little Flying Lady" thanks to her motorized paraglider hobby.

Despite the "little lady" moniker, however, Shiina was a fine mother in her own right with a child in high school. Misuzu got the feeling that between the two of them, Shiina was actually older than she was, but her toned skin and the way water flicked off it was nothing to shake a stick at. Even now, she wore a graceful—well, it *looked* graceful, but there were spots on it here and there that were fairly aggressive—white one-piece bathing suit, and her arms and legs brimmed with the vitality of a teenager.

"At it again, Mrs. Kamijou?"

"Yes. You would be surprised at how much lung capacity you need for a hobby like mine."

Misuzu, who was casually glancing at her upper arms, thighs, and so on, began to groan to herself at Shiina's body—it was virtually impeccable.

...*Ugh, that's so frustrating. What kind of stretches do you need to do to look so fresh and vibrant?*

Still, Misuzu was a beauty in her own right. She was right at home among the other students at university lectures. But she knew. She was fully aware of all the unspoken words people thought when they described her beauty or youthful looks: beautiful (at a glance, but actually, you see...), so young-looking (for someone with a child), the spitting image of a university student (even though she's so much older)... She knew that the monster named "age" had opened its gaping mouth and was even now trying to swallow her whole as she madly dashed away from it!!

From Misuzu's point of view, she had little choice but to be envious of what she saw in Shiina.

And because she put in all that effort, she understood another thing: Shiina Kamijou, despite being older than her, didn't put in any effort like that whatsoever. The woman had unfading beauty to spare.

Even now, with a lighthearted "Here we go!" or some such thing, she simply drifted away, like a corpse in the water, her face under the surface with both hands gripping a kickboard all the while.

...*I might as well have Mikoto recommend me a crazy health machine from Academy City or something. Wait, no. If I'm on a regular diet, the fat and stuff that makes my skin shine will go away, too, which would leave me all dried out...*

Misuzu, incessantly muttering at the water's surface, went along with Shiina to the poolside after the latter was fully satisfied with a round of what looked like pretending to drown.

"I gotta say," said Misuzu, "it's surprisingly carefree and easy living alone as a housewife, huh? Though I guess I only have the luxury of saying that because I know he'll come back on a regular basis."

"Oh, Mrs. Misaka, does your husband work abroad by himself?"

"Working abroad…though I'm not entirely sure *what* it is he does. I essentially have no idea where he is or what he's up to right now."

"My husband doesn't work alone, but he does go on overseas business trips quite a lot. And every single time, he brings back these strange souvenirs he's bought. There are times when I wonder if he actually ends up in mysterious, unexplored lands."

Misuzu and Shiina shared a laugh.

…They didn't know that, in reality, the two husbands they were talking about (plus Tanaka, a new employee, as well as others they'd met on their travels) really were running around the world getting themselves into heaps of trouble.

Wiping off with a long towel, Shiina abruptly said, "By the way, I've heard that the school my son goes to is canceling its midterm exams."

"Hmm? Oh—yeah, now that you mention it, it's the same for my Mikoto. I think she said their second-semester grades are going to depend entirely on their final exams. Still, I doubt she feels pressure from that, so I'm sure things will go the same as they always do."

"As for my Touma, I'm sure that whether things are going the same or not, he'll end up failing and needing to take supplementary classes."

The two of them shared a laugh together, but then Misuzu suddenly realized something.

"…It looks like we certainly *talk* like mothers at least, huh?"

"Oh, but it would seem we *are* model housewives."

A girl passing by, who looked like a student, gave them a confused look, but, well, that was how things usually went.

"Hmm…" Misuzu thought for a moment. "There *has* been one minor thing on my mind for a little while."

"What is it?"

"Our children are studying over in Academy City, right? And they're borrowing its top-of-the-line scientific technological expertise to nurture supernatural powers as well, right?"

"Yes, I believe so," said Shiina, silently mouthing the words *Though I'm not sure about Touma...*

"I wonder what decides if you have the potential for supernatural abilities."

"Oh, well, I must say, I don't know much about those things... But I would assume it comes down to genetics, or DNA, or something like that, wouldn't it?"

"Right, probably." Misuzu nodded. "But that would mean..."

"Hmm?"

"Well. I was just wondering, if Mikoto was able to become Academy City's third-ranked Level Five, then if I took the same kind of curriculum as her, maybe I'd have sparks and electricity coming out of my bangs, too."

"Oh my!" cried out Shiina in elegant surprise.

Misuzu's words continued to flow, perhaps because they were both parents who had left their children in Academy City's care. "...Sometimes I wonder if people like that are all over the world. It gives me a strange feeling. Like, Mikoto might be in third place, but maybe there's people with even better talents just hanging around somewhere and nobody would ever know..."

The last part of her sentence trailed off, like she was talking to herself.

Maybe there were people in the world who never realized their own talents and ended up living average housewife lives forever. Or maybe there were other people who had convinced themselves they were normal despite unconsciously using mysterious powers on a daily basis.

Maybe those powers weren't the easily seen kind, like making fire come out of your hands or having lightning bolts shoot out of your bangs. Just little things that went unnoticed in day-to-day life—like people with better-than-average gut instincts or people who could write letters better than most, or people who looked a little younger than their actual age—silly, trivial anomalies like those. Maybe there was some kind of theory or rule set behind it all, and everyone lived with their very own special powers all the time.

"Oh, well!" said Shiina. "Why not enroll at an Academy City university and find out?"

"Hmm. That sounds like it would be fun, but at my age, I don't think I could participate in an Ability Development curriculum," said Misuzu with a laugh. "In the end, we'll never know the truth. But maybe that's what keeps the mystery in life, huh?"

CHAPTER 17

B Movies and Unpolished, Uncut Gemstones
First Friday of October

Shiage Hamazura, having quit Skill-Out due to certain circumstances, now did menial labor for a minor organization in Academy City's underworld called Item. The small team was made up of just four members, but it was apparently a group to be reckoned with nonetheless, and he got the feeling they were receiving a large budget from *somewhere*.

This particular story began with one of that mysterious organization's members, Saiai Kinuhata, a girl of about twelve years, asking an offhand question.

"Hamazura, Hamazura," she said. "Can you get an ID for me like *super-mega*-fast?"

"I once led over a hundred people in Skill-Out, even if it was just temporarily," grumbled Hamazura. "Why should I have to do dumb little errands like that...?"

"You're being *super*-complainy right now—so, the ID?"

"Damn it. That's a demand, isn't it? You're *ordering* me to make one. Well, I can throw together a smart card pretty quick, but passports and stuff like that would take a while."

Hamazura was a criminal through and through. At no point in their conversation did he ever say he *couldn't* do it.

Kinuhata waved her small hands to reassure him. "Oh, uh, they don't have to be, like, super-intricate or anything. I just want to fake my age, so it can just be, like, a high school student ID or something."

Hamazura was baffled. "What the heck do you want something like that for?"

"It's for a super extremely important mission," Kinuhata began, acting like explaining all this was a massive chore. "It's so I can watch a PG-13 movie coming out next week!!"

And that was how Hamazura's first job of his second life began.

Watching movies was Saiai Kinuhata's hobby. She loved movies spanning many different genres and qualities. However, she was only fanatical about the kinds of movies that elicited reactions like *I've never heard of those* or worse, make people say *What...is that...?*

"Wait, I didn't know there was a theater around here...?"

"It's only B grade this time. And if you want B movies, this is totally the place to go. If you want to go all the way to C movies, though, you have to go even deeper."

"Ehhh...," groaned Hamazura.

They veered off a main road onto a smaller one, then onto a lane that branched out from that, then found a building that looked like one of those multipurpose structures, except squashed down from above.

The theater was buried in a very densely populated area; even satellites would have had a tough time spotting anything. Apparently, this was a location known only to Kinuhata. It was, of course, a theater specializing in movies that only aired in a single location—a unique place where the clientele was assaulted by obscure works that would never see the light of day ever again after this airing. A facility of indie terror that would put amateurs into a coma.

Kinuhata put her hands on her hips, then exhaled. She seemed to be psyching herself up. "We have the ID now, but there's one more thing I want in order to touch up my appearance. If we both show the same IDs *together*, we'll totally be able to fool the ticket lady."

After one thing or another, they managed to slip past the intelligent-looking librarian-type ticket lady's cautious gaze and infiltrated the theater. They proceeded down the dirty hallways, which made the place look like a mansion in a horror game, then opened a pair of double doors to step into the screening room beyond.

The building was small to begin with, but the screening room was even tinier. It was like a school auditorium, only bigger, and even the multilevel seating somewhat resembled a university lecture room, the kind you'd see on TV.

But there was something odder than that.

"...Hey. This movie opens today, and you can't see it anywhere in Japan except for here, right? How is this place completely empty fifteen minutes before it starts?"

"Ahhhn! ☆"

When he got some weird heavy breathing in response to his question, Hamazura turned a blank face on his companion. The girl looked like she was about to swoon—her legs were wobbling, and both her hands were pressed to her cheeks.

"I'm the only one on opening day for a movie you can only see right here. That means I'm the only one who understands how *super*-wonderful this work will be!! Yes, I know, it's all an illusion. But right here, in this moment alone, I will be the only one experiencing what the honored director wants to convey with his film!!"

The airhead seemed to have gone off on her own weird journey by herself, so Hamazura left her there for a minute to buy some popcorn. When he came back to the seats in the very middle of the theater, Kinuhata looked at his popcorn and laughed down her nose at him.

"Heh. I thought you would have understood what a folly caramel popcorn is—it'll make your throat super-dry in the middle of the movie. You really don't get it, do you, Hamazura?"

"Then quit reaching in and scarfing down even more than me. Look, I got drinks, too."

"Oh, you think *that* will be enough? Out of all the things, you chose a large carbonated drink. What are you going to do when you have to go to the bathroom in the middle of the movie? Hamazura, you really are a *total* Hamazura after all, I suppose."

"Says the one holding her carbonated drink tight while swinging her legs around under her seat…"

In the meantime, the lights in the theater dimmed. There was a soft electric hum, and then the screen lit up. Ordinary movies usually started with a stream of around ten minutes of previews from the distribution company, but this feature film started right away. It was like they were so strapped—for various things—that they couldn't even introduce any other movies.

As he glanced at the title card that came up, which looked like paper someone had cut up and pasted directly onto the film—in the era of full digital movies, no less!—Hamazura asked lamely, "Hey, uh…"

"What is it, Hamazura, that is so important that you interrupt me during what is totally the greatest moment of my life?"

"…Thirty seconds in, and the screen is already filled with frenzied zombies who literally just have their faces painted blue-green. How am I supposed to react to this?"

"You totally don't understand how to enjoy B movies, do you?" said Kinuhata back. As she helped herself to the popcorn without asking, she prefaced that usually talking was banned inside movie theaters, but she'd make an exception. "Listen here. All B movies look super-shabby. These are people with no money or manpower *desperate* to make something. There might be a few exceptions, but there's really no surefire way to make them look impressive."

"Then why would they bother cramming so many economy-class seats in a tiny movie theater? Wouldn't it be better to see the huge Hollywood hits in one of the really big theaters?"

"Do you really think so? It might come as a surprise, but the movies everyone calls B and C are more likely to be diamonds in the rough and can surprisingly stick with you longer than the big hits that come out every month and constantly break records over and over. Even while you're complaining about how totally stupid one of these movies is, the next thing you know, you're super-engaged."

"Right… I don't really get it."

Hamazura sighed. As he thought, it didn't help at all asking someone why something was interesting when they enjoyed it from the get-go. It felt like someone was explaining, at length, what was so great about a band he wasn't that into.

B and C movies are diamonds in the rough compared to most big works, eh…?

Maybe that was something these movies and people had in common, he mused to himself.

The world was filled with people of all sorts of different talents. How many of them were given a chance to properly express those abilities, though? How many unused abilities had been buried, unbeknownst even to their owners who lacked the massive budgets, capable mentors, and the equipment and facilities needed to make full use of them?

Shiage Hamazura, for example, had received a Level Zero rating, but that could have just been an issue with how the teachers were nurturing his talents. Saiai Kinuhata, for example, might have had an ability she could healthily express if she went somewhere that had more sunlight. Academy City only had seven Level Five espers in it—but was that really all? The world outside the city was big. There could be an eighth or a ninth, their talents lying dormant and undiscovered, working as street-side flower vendors or something.

When he thought about it like that, it started to make a little more sense how this magnum-wielding detective shooting away at the green zombies on this tiny little theater screen really did represent a challenge to how much inequality existed in the world. Maybe he was simply declaring that even if he'd been denied the place and destiny to fully exercise his own talents, he was still enjoying his life more than anyone else on this planet?

"……"

The information from the screen transformed into a sprawling scene in Hamazura's mind.

He *did* feel like those sorts of revelations changed the way he viewed works like this. Rather than a depressing sense of sympathy, it was more like an odd understanding. What was there right now wasn't entirely interesting, but it did let him *think* it would get more interesting as it went along. It was a strange feeling: not quite trust, not quite excitement. Just an uninterrupted desire to follow this director's future works.

Was this what drew Kinuhata to these movies?

He gave her a casual, sidelong glance. She didn't notice how his gaze rested on her face, which was illuminated by the reflection from the screen. Her expression was solemn in a way, single-mindedly homed in on the screen.

And then, she abruptly opened her mouth and said:

"Ugh. This is *super*-boring."

A moment later, with a *wham*, Hamazura fell out of his chair headfirst, spilling the caramel popcorn all over the floor.

"Wha—*heeeeeeeeeeeeeeeeeeeeeeeeeeeeeey*!! *You're* the one who forced me to forge you an ID and dragged *me* here to watch this film no one's even heard of before!! You're the one who was in the lead, waving her movie-loving flag around—at least *pretend* to be enjoying this!!"

"That's strange. When I read the pamphlet, it seemed like it would be super-interesting. But about ten minutes in, I realized it hadn't really grabbed me. I suppose you have to see movies in person to really know for sure. How very profound…"

"Whoa, hang on a second. What the hell was that weird sense of understanding and a willingness to identify with B movies that was beginning to sprout inside me?!"

"What are you talking about? There's no way a shitty movie like this could ever teach you anything. And besides, I highly doubt *you* have any idea how to properly enjoy B movies yet."

"…?!" Feeling like she'd pulled one over on him, the doorway to movies in Hamazura's heart slammed shut.

As if intent on running down a fleeing enemy, Kinuhata yawned and said, "Well, the heroine is totally going to die in about twenty minutes. The whole staff has been dropping hints for a while now that they *really* want to kill her off already."

"Wow, you're not even slightly invested!! Y-you know what, no! I say she won't die!! That heroine is going to survive the zombie apocalypse and witness the dawn of a new day together with the protagonist!"

"Wanna bet? I'll bet a stick of gum she totally dies."

"She won't die!! As a matter of fact, I'm practically *obsessed* with this tight-lipped, brave heroine!!"

Right after he said that, the screen showed the single female member of the team getting killed and eaten. It wasn't instant death, but her skin rapidly lost its color, and she was wearing an expression that just begged for a background of flower petals scattering in the wind.

Hamazura held his head in his hands.

"Yes, the gum's mine!" Kinuhata said resolutely, her voice reverberating through the theater.

When going to a movie, always go with someone who will stay until the credits roll.

CHAPTER 18
Befitting to Inherit the Name

First Friday of October

"Lord Hanzou, I've finally found you," whispered the shinobi girl all wrapped in chains.

This was the aboveground portion of School District 22. Unlike the other districts, almost 100 percent of city functions here were provided by underground facilities. The surface was entirely covered with various wind turbines. Steel bars crisscrossed like jungle gyms, piled up to thirty stories high, with three-dimensional arrangements of propellers here and there generating power from the wind.

One young man with a bandanna around his head stood alone in the center of that uncanny, propeller-filled scenery.

It was Hanzou, leaning against a vertical support beam as he leveled his gaze on the girl, Kuruwa, who was wearing a yellow mini-yukata that was transparent around the waist.

"I cannot *believe* you would fake your identity, sneak into the city, and then chase me around for almost half a year," said Hanzou. "What's driving you to go this far?"

"A restoration. Of the noble and upright house of the Hattori—and furthermore, for the rise of the Iga," she answered smoothly.

But Hanzou, upon hearing that, sighed in disbelief. "You don't actually know what a shinobi is, do you?"

"......"

"If you go far back enough, it's clear they started out as bandits, hired by some big-shot military commander or other. Couldn't be further from *noble and upright houses*. Some of them were granted titles later, sure, but the further back you trace our roots, the clearer it becomes that we were the kind of nobodies you can find just about anywhere."

Hanzou shoved both hands into his pockets, then continued, "Listen to me, Kuruwa. A shinobi's rightful place is as the weeds, as the skittering vermin, as the supporting players... As soon as you start talking about *noble and upright houses*, you won't be able to survive in this world. And do you know why not? If those of us meant to hide in the dark shine just a little too brightly, a blink of an eye later and we'll all be dead from a focused strike."

"That is nothing but evidence that those who roost in high places truly fear the shinobi. But we have entered a new age, an era in which we must begin to act in more efficient ways."

She really wants a place to call home that badly, huh? Hanzou shook his head. The saddest thing was that even though he considered her an idiot, he *did* understand where she was coming from.

"I'm telling you this for your own sake," he said. "Learn from the weeds. Heed the wisdom of vermin. Respect the supporting players. Weeds are everywhere. Vermin never go away. And supporting players blend in with the scenery. Equipping oneself with all these things and distilling them, concentrating them... *That* is the way of the shinobi."

"Shall we never understand one another?"

"Not so long as people don't endeavor *to* understand."

"Fine, then. In that case..."

He heard a *click* from inside Kuruwa's right sleeve. She only had one; her left arm was exposed up to the shoulder. She made a slight motion, and the chains enveloping her jingled.

"I shall cease my attempts at persuasion," she continued. "I shall *force* you to surrender, then use you to craft a tool for my personal quest to restore the Hattori."

"That's a pretty radical way to propose. Did you want to have children or something?"

"Yes, indeed, if it is also necessary. By force, if need be."

Hanzou couldn't help but sigh at how seriously she said that. "Planning on taking out a gun?"

"I... No, I've abandoned such things... I was told they aren't very fitting for a shinobi..."

"?"

"Er, more importantly, although the mechanisms within firearms are complex, there are techniques that effectively render such mechanisms unstable."

Hanzou, confused by all this, listened as Kuruwa tried her best to speak calmly.

"In fact, there are some models which will malfunction should their magazine become twisted by even a mere millimeter. Against you, Lord Hanzou, I believe it best for me to face you with a simple weapon instead."

Clang!!

A loud metallic noise resounded, and a thirty-centimeter-long sickle appeared from Kuruwa's sleeve. She removed the chains around her body, then attached the sickle to one end. On the other end was the metal shackle bound to her ankle.

"A chain and sickle, eh?" Hanzou asked with his hands still buried in his pants pockets as he narrowed his eyes. "Not a true weapon of the shinobi... Unconventional and concealable but too conspicuous."

"......"

Kuruwa didn't respond to the attempt at conversation.

However, it wasn't that she tried to crush him without giving him time to speak:

Voom!!

No, it was because Hanzou's body was suddenly right beside Kuruwa's.

She gasped, but by the time Kuruwa tried to back away, Hanzou had already taken the last step up to her. His right hand, which had been in his pants pocket, had come out at some point. And it was drawn back into a fist.

However, the light caught something up his sleeve.

The moment she realized it was a sharp edge, Hanzou's fingers were already flying at her face.

"?!"

It was so fast that only her neck was able to react, which she just barely managed to swing out of the path of danger.

"A dart...!!"

"This is what real shinobi use."

In his hand, Hanzou held an extremely short arrow, about fifteen centimeters long. This one was specifically designed for stabbing rather than throwing. An assassin's tool, sometimes called the world's smallest short spear.

For Hanzou's next thrust, Kuruwa was forced to coil her chains around her hand and use them to block. The primary use of a chain and sickle was to rely on centrifugal force and throw the weighted end of the chain at an enemy to entangle their weapons and limbs, leaving them vulnerable to attack with the sickle. But with rapid blows coming in such close quarters, Kuruwa didn't have time to swing the chain around and get it up to speed.

Forced into a defensive battle, Kuruwa ground her teeth.

Hanzou wasn't being serious about this. A true shinobi would have made sure to kill her in the first exchange. And if he'd failed, he'd have immediately escaped. But he wasn't playing this by the book—did he intend to pin her down and settle this peacefully?

"You have...underestimated me a fair bit...!!"

Abandoning her respectful tone toward her senior, Kuruwa kept part of the chain taut with both hands and swung the rest of it. The attack had no curve to it and ended up more like a jab, and Hanzou veered his head away to dodge it.

Kuruwa took advantage of that opening to put distance between them.

She dove behind a steel pillar for the wind-power generators, possibly meaning to keep some cover between them.

"...!!"

Hanzou immediately surged forward. Without giving Kuruwa

time to rally, he wheeled around the pillar, using his momentum to deliver a ferocious roundhouse attack. The tip of his dart thrust forward to slash through the fluttering yellow fabric.

But then his face darkened.

The only thing there was her yukata, which she'd stripped off and left behind.

A loud *whoosh* shot through the air.

Hanzou's attention homed in on the sound. Kuruwa had manuevered around the beam in the other direction, mirroring his own steps. Stripped down to her underwear, she bought herself a fraction of a second to swing her chain. It formed a circle with a one-meter radius. She swung the chain around two more times, then a third. Hanzou, seeing the speed and energy the weight was gaining, heard his body scream danger.

Here it comes!!

She would be trying to tie down his weapon with the chain, and, with his movements sealed, she would close in on him with her sickle at the ready.

Fortunately for Hanzou, the chain and sickle were easy to predict. Because the wielder needed to whip the chain around in circles to build up energy, they had to let go at just the right angle at just the right time or else the weighted end would fly off in the wrong direction.

A revolving weight and an unmistakable sound splitting the air.

As Hanzou concentrated on these two things, he heard a much louder *whoosh* filling his ears.

I just have to—?!

He shifted his center of gravity to dodge sideways, but then he noticed something.

Kuruwa still hadn't let go of the chain.

The whooshing noise had been nothing more than Kuruwa making the sound with her own mouth as a feint.

"Shi—"

He'd noticed the ruse, but now that he was already leaning in one direction, he couldn't immediately shift in the other. Thanks to his hesitation, he ended up freezing in place and not moving at all. This time, the chain hurtled toward him, ready to take his life.

The moment she flung the weighted end of the chain, Kuruwa knew that she had won.

Hanzou wouldn't be able to dodge this blow. The thick chain would coil around his right arm, preventing him from moving. After that, she only had to yank the chain, throw her opponent off-balance, and dive in for the finishing blow.

She knew she had a decisive advantage, but somewhere inside, she still felt something akin to loneliness.

In the end, was this all Hanzou's strength—and that of the Hattori family—amounted to?

She gritted her teeth, but her chain flew true.

It soared in between his side and his elbow, then wrapped around his arm like a snake—

Fwoom!!
—and then it slipped through his arm entirely, flying off into the distance.

"Huh…?"

Kuruwa, pulled by the unforeseen direction of the chain, ended up leaning slightly forward.

The chain should have wrapped around Hanzou's arm, but instead it had gone right *through* it, like it had hit a sheet of paper. It took Kuruwa a moment to actually realize what had happened.

Hanzou's right arm flapped.

Or rather, his arm was no longer in the long, flapping sleeve. Kuruwa had aimed for his arm but had hit nothing but the fabric of his sleeve.

Hanzou's right arm was probably scrunched up inside his shirt.

He couldn't stab with a dart like that.

However…

That didn't mean he had only one weapon.

Whoosh!! Hanzou bolted forward. Though Kuruwa immediately tried to block him with her chain, she couldn't move the way she wanted to since the chain had missed and pulled her body along with it.

She was only off balance for a fraction of a second.

But that was enough for Hanzou to press the advantage.

"A..."

And in that moment, Kuruwa was, for some reason, smiling.

As she watched the finishing blow drawing nearer, the girl who wished for the restoration of the Hattori clan was practically beaming.

"Amazing, Lord Hanzou!!"

Something glinted in Hanzou's left hand.

Hanzou quietly peered down at the collapsed woman.

Lying there in nothing but her underwear, she wasn't bleeding badly. At the last second, Hanzou had pulled back the dart in his hand and merely punched her instead.

"...Sheesh. That's a pretty happy expression for someone who just got beaten up," Hanzou scoffed, clicking his tongue.

The way she lived wasn't in line with the secret teachings of the shinobi. The kind of mindset that strove for a singular purpose even if it meant death—that was something he'd thought was reserved for those following the Bushido code, intent on protecting peace and order in Japan.

He could never live like that.

Shinobi were like the weeds—like vermin: just supporting characters. In the end, even after one friend named Komaba had died and another friend named Hamazura had been lost to him, he'd been living the same life as always, just on his own.

Ninjas certainly weren't strong or admirable.

As the previous battle attested, the secret behind the ninja arts was to use subtle tricks to tip the flow of battle in your favor, then take advantage of it to launch an attack at the opponent's blind spot.

Therefore, Hanzou, who wasn't a special person by any means, never engaged in any combat where he couldn't kill an enemy in a single blow with absolute certainty. And that habit was a fundamental characteristic of anyone who lived their life as a spy—he understood that.

It's so sickening, though...

Hanzou shook his head and collected the mini-yukata Kuruwa had left behind. She was a kunoichi who had learned that technique, but he didn't have the heart to just leave her lying on the ground half naked. He spread the mini-yukata over the unconscious young woman like a sheet.

"......"

But then, he felt paper rustle.

He fished around a little inside the sleeve; he found a short report.

A list...of Uncut Gems...?

Natural espers were a minor rumor even in Academy City. Was Kuruwa planning on making them her allies and creating a new team of ninjas or something?

Sure, strictly speaking, shinobi were creatures of science. And unlike Hanzou, Kuruwa wanted a flashy, grand, noble group of ninjutsu users. From that point of view, simply having a unit composed of nothing but Uncut Gems must have been pretty appealing in its own right.

But Hanzou was frowning for a different reason.

He thought to himself quietly, the list of Uncut Gems in his hand.

...Why does Kuruwa have a top secret Academy City document like this?

Kuruwa was descended from the shinobi, but she'd also taken close to half a year to catch Hanzou. She couldn't have been very skilled in the art of acquiring information from across a large region, even if she *was* good at blending into the scenery and sneaking through large crowds.

Whoever made this list is using Kuruwa to try to accomplish their own goals. But who? And what are they after?

He thought about it for a while but couldn't come up with an answer.

...What the hell is going on in this city anyway?

He crumpled the report in his hand.

CHAPTER 19

Shining Uncut Gems and Bloodied Concessions
Second Friday of October

Every last one of these damn Academy City General Board members was a rich asshole, and it frustrated Seria Kumokawa to no end.

Looking around the home theater that Tsugutoshi Kaizumi had personally created for himself, girl genius Seria found herself pressing a finger to her temple once more at the inequity of it all.

The room was dome shaped—ill-suited for a private residence—and while she'd dubbed it a home theater, the space put a lot of store in acoustics. Clusters of speakers surrounded her in every direction, filling every last bit of available wall space, so painstakingly arranged that they were even installed on the back of the door.

"One of my acquaintances is a professional conductor, you see," said an old man in full dress who would be more at home among antique equipment. "I decided I'd let his obsession with live performances run wild, and so he did one thing and another, and the next thing I knew, he'd created *this*. My wife and daughter were just as astonished."

"Not that I care about *any* of that, but you'd need to create some pretty specialized music data to make use of this many speakers."

"Indeed. The sound quality is heavenly, but each song costing twenty million yen *is* a bit of a fly in the ointment."

"I hope you die," spat Kumokawa, glancing at the theater's large monitor. *That* was no cheapskate projector. It was a super-high-resolution display easily over three hundred inches. With one of these, you could buy an entire theater *and* the land it sat on.

And it was *not* showing a big hit movie that would be forgotten within a year.

No—all there was to see was the face of a sorry excuse for a man.

Kumokawa took a seat in a leather chair that was so soft, one could slip into eternal slumber while sitting in it. Then, taking a drink from the side table, she looked back at the screen.

"I hate the profiteering business, but this place is at least sound-proofed enough for us to speak in secret," she said, pausing. "I suppose I'll deign to listen to your trivial grievances now."

"I…I haven't done anything I'd need to make excuses for," said the giant face displayed on the screen. "And I find it a bother to explain this, but we aren't involved in this matter. Go ahead—look into it. This string of actions occurred spontaneously, without our involvement."

"I see," said Kaizumi, placing a hand on the back of the chair Kumokawa was sitting in. "Then you're saying you have *nothing* to do with the Uncut Gems in France, India, Australia, Thailand, Argentina, and other places around the world suddenly all being sought after for research samples?"

"That's right." The man on the screen nodded. "It's true that in the past, we developed and executed projects like Stargate with serious aspirations to put espers to military use. But not this time. If you investigate the composition of all these organizations, you'll understand. There's no connection between them. And they're not groups created with our investments."

"Indeed," said Kumokawa, taking a sip of the pink-colored liquid through a straw. She glanced at the documents sitting on the side table. Assembled like a variety of fruits, they were investigative reports on the groups who were now making passes at the Uncut Gems.

"They're many things," she said. "Academic organizations, scientific think tanks, sports engineering groups, and even a somewhat odd human trafficking ring. There certainly isn't any evidence that there's any networking between them, and they also don't seem to be using *you* as a shield."

"Of course not. However famous the CIA might be, you can't just pin the blame on us for every conspiracy you find in the world."

"I'd think not. By the way, I had a little question for you." Kumokawa tossed the papers aside. "Academic organizations, scientific think tanks, sports engineering groups, somewhat odd human trafficking rings... Each of them has been infiltrated by *two* of your vaunted CIA spies. What is the meaning of that?"

"?!"

"Did you think we wouldn't notice? You have, in fact, *personally* created a network distributed throughout all these independent groups." Kumokawa frowned. "But why? As the brains behind your country, this sort of methodology isn't the thing I'd think you'd want to use."

The man on the screen began denying the allegations vehemently, but Kumokawa ignored him and ended the call.

Kaizumi looked down at the crown of her head. "What do you think?"

"Well," said Kumokawa, shaking her glass to spin the ice in it around a bit. "The individual organizations aren't a worry. However they decide to mess around with the Uncut Gems, they'll never be able to get their hands on any Ability Development technology that would put them to practical use. If they're just going to fail on their own regardless, we can leave them alone."

"......"

"Still, the Stargate people will probably try to acquire all the data gathered from their collective failures and aggregate it. Failure begets success and all that—they might make progress by using all those failures to narrow things down."

"What is the risk of that, in concrete numbers?"

"Hmm," replied Kumokawa airily.

"Zero percent. It's not a worry."

Kaizumi sucked in a breath.

It wasn't relief—it was more like mild amazement. He'd probably predicted this.

Kumokawa continued, "Even if they go that far, they'll fail. They won't know how to apply the data they gather in practical applications, and they'll end up deadlocked. But as long as they don't realize their failure, they'll probably keep expending their Uncut Gems."

"I see. Then we have no more trivial concerns," said Kaizumi briefly. And then, he ventured, "Let's get to the main subject... What do we do now?"

"Hmph. Naïve as always, I see."

"I understand that each of those groups will fail on their own. But I don't like them expending Uncut Gems while they're doing it... Actually, I'll stop referring to them as that. The people whose lives are threatened right now are just children who happen to have predominantly minor talents."

Capture operations might have already been under way. If they wanted to secure the Uncut Gem children unharmed, they'd have to move decisively before those other organizations began their research in earnest. In any case, though all these various groups styled themselves "research organizations," realistically, they possessed almost zero relevant knowledge or technology when it came to Ability Development. Biased by their beliefs and preconceptions, it wouldn't have been surprising even if they ended up dissecting the children as soon as they captured them before preserving them in formaldehyde.

"I thought I'd already answered that question," answered Kumokawa, annoyed. "Only fifty or so Uncut Gems even exist. But countless weirdo scientists are after them. That means it would be faster to deal with the *Uncut Gems* instead."

"......"

"Invite them to Academy City. It would be the most efficient way of guaranteeing their safety. You are the one who argued that those children have their own lives to live, or something along those lines, and then did nothing. We're on the back foot now thanks to your kindness."

"I admit my error," said Kaizumi in a hard voice. "But I still submit that you, the brain, are making an impossible request. When you get right down to it, what do we *do*? They're immediately going to work off the Uncut Gems list that the CIA put together without our input, then start mining for the children nearby. Even if we dispatched people from Academy City right now, they wouldn't make it in time when everywhere else in the world is starting the mining process at the same time. Do you have a plan to get around this?"

"It's true that dispatching people from Academy City *alone* won't be enough. Even using supersonic passenger planes, there are geographical limitations to consider."

"However," she added plainly, "the situation changes if we use the groups cooperating with Academy City around the world. If our rivals are simultaneously stirring the pot across the globe, then all we have to do is take action against them on the same scale."

"You say it like it's so easy," objected Kaizumi. "They may be cooperating with us, but none of them are as powerful as you seem to be suggesting. Most of them are corporations we've made business agreements with and groups who supply us with resources and the like. I can count on my fingers the number of them with military assets that we could entrust with a request potentially involving violence. It would be impossible for them alone to secure the fifty or so Uncut Gems right away."

Academy City could indirectly control almost all of modern society that relied on science, but the indirect nature of that relationship meant orders were carried out slowly, and there were not a great many fast response options available. "Get all the military in the world to act right now" was not a card they conveniently had in hand.

"Well, that's how it appears on the surface," said Kumokawa.

"?"

"I'd rather not place myself in *his* debt, but we should swallow our pride and ask that frog for help."

"What are you talking about, exactly?"

"What?" Kumokawa drained the rest of her glass's contents through her straw, then smiled. "I'm just saying we should ask a bunch of girls who all share the same face to do the fighting for us."

CHAPTER 20
A Response to Multiple Simultaneous Tragedies
Second Friday of October

It is time for regularly scheduled reports.

"*Reporting from the Church of High-Order Contact in Galashiels, Scotland: Confirmed suppression of domes number four, eight, and thirteen, reports Misaka number 17000.*"

"*Reporting from the World Intellectual Club in Lausanne, Switzerland: Misaka has eliminated armed security personnel, says Misaka number 18022, beginning verification process.*"

"*Reporting from the Sixth Sense Headquarters in Guadalajara, Mexico: Misaka has destroyed the main door to the research building, says Misaka number 14333, venturing farther inside.*"

"*Reporting from the Center for Living-Body Sports Analysis in Puerto Deseado, Argentina: Misaka has gained control over electronic security locks, says Misaka number 15110, opening up a route to the top secret area.*"

"*Reporting from the main headquarters of the Wisdom of Mankind in Davao, Philippines: Misaka has confirmed the departure of an escape vessel and is settling the issue before they can flee, says Misaka number 10090, commencing an attack.*"

Zzz...

...Zzzzz, zzz...

...Zhhhh...zzz.

"*Reporting from the main offices of Blueprint of the Gods in*

Ahmednagar, India: Destruction of blocks A, D, and L complete, says Misaka number 12053, continuing the operation."

"Reporting from the Council of Mankind's Evolution in Beijing, China: An attack helicopter has appeared, says Misaka number 19009, heaving an unserious sigh."

"Reporting from the Special Energy Institute in La Paragua, Venezuela: Misaka has successfully destroyed eight percent of research equipment, says Misaka number 11899, still swamped with work to do."

"Reporting from the Mental Universe Research Division in Moosonee, Canada: Severance of all electrical sources, including emergency power generators, is now complete, reports Misaka number 16836 from complete darkness."

"Reporting from the International Bank of Superior Genetics in Salzburg, Austria: Misaka has discovered a little white kitten, but now isn't the time for that, says Misaka number 10502, tearing herself away from it and returning to battle."

Ba-bam!!

Rat-tat-tat-tat! Bang-bang!! Bang!!

Booom!!

"Reporting from the Extraterrestrial Chaos Observation Station at the South Pole: Here comes a counterattack, says Misaka number 19900, responding to the aggression."

"Reporting from the OOPArts Historical Archive in Chiang Mai, Thailand: At current threat levels, Misaka should be able to manage this on her own, evaluates Misaka number 12083."

"Reporting from the Council of Anti-Radio Wave Salvation in Starogard, Poland: It seems this is the last of the resistance, reports Misaka number 10855, in what she hopes is an uninterested manner."

"Reporting from the Wings Toward the Future's central core in Faenza, Italy: Well, there are tanks all over the place causing trouble for Misaka here, says Misaka number 17203, fed up with this."

"Reporting from the Precision Microfaith Church in Logroño, Spain: Some sort of military dropout assassin has appeared, says Misaka number 19488, crushing the enemy with a swift assault."

Clack!!

Boom!! Zhh-bm-bm-bm-bm-bm-bm!!

Fweeeeeeeeeeee!!

"Reporting from the Cutting-Edge Scientific Institute in Kunsan, South Korea: Misaka has arrested all main research personnel, reports Misaka number 15327."

"Reporting from the National Institute for the Analysis of Oneiromancy in Angoulême, France: Misaka has been given a comment that she will come to rue this day, says Misaka number 13072, blowing them up regardless."

"Reporting from the Global Awakening Federation in Codajás, Brazil: Misaka is leaving processing the arrested masterminds for later and hurrying on ahead, says Misaka number 17403, advancing into the innermost sanctum."

"Reporting from the Brain Distribution Explication Center in Zacapa, Guatemala: No resistance here, so Misaka will secure the Uncut Gem, says Misaka number 10050, heading for research building seven."

"Reporting from the Paranormal Introduction Dictionary in Salzgitter, Germany: Misaka has located a hidden door, says Misaka number 10840, peering inside."

Slide.

…Tap…tap…

Squeak, squeak.

"Reporting from the Neo Energy Mining Organization in Celje, Slovenia: Uncut Gem located, reports Misaka number 12481."

"Reporting from the Evidence for Overlords in Bergen, Norway: This Misaka has also located an Uncut Gem, reports Misaka number 18072."

"Reporting from the Ecliptic Access Line Popularization Council in Rovaniemi, Finland: beginning to secure the Uncut Gem, says Misaka number 19348, reaching out her hand to offer help."

"Reporting from the Cryptid Ecology Elucidation Club in Sydney, Australia: Confirmed escape route; now exiting the facility with the Uncut Gem, says Misaka number 17009, moving."

"Reporting from the Seventh Generation Weapons Institute in Bragança, Portugal: Escape successful and safety of the Uncut Gem confirmed, says Misaka number 15113 with a sigh of relief."

No.

It's too early to be relieved, reports Misaka number 10032 urgently!!

"Wha—? Isn't number 10032 supposed to be in Academy City? asks Misaka number 14014."

"An emergency report from there—what do you mean by that? asks Misaka number 18829, requesting an explanation."

We have an invader. Number: one.

Their aim seems to be Academy City's strongest Uncut Gem: The number seven Level Five, adds Misaka number 10032 onto her report!!

Zz.

Zhh...zhh...zh.

Zhhzhzhhzhzhzhhzhzhzhhhzhhhhhhzhzh!!

CHAPTER 21

Those Whose Identities Cannot Be Discerned
Second Friday of October

It was a strange sight to behold.

School District 11: The district where all the shipping containers were held. Nothing but giant boxes made of metal lined these streets—and among them lay about nine girls, all defeated. Everything about them was identical, from their clothing to their hair, from their heights to their builds, even right down to the composition of their faces. They were the Sisters, created from a certain Level Five's somatic cells.

Strewn about were rifles, scattered bullet casings, and the girls themselves, limp and unconscious. In the middle of them all stood a single man.

Unharmed.

The man who should have become a magic god, Ollerus, narrowed his eyes as the night breeze blew over him.

He was on the run from the entire sorcery world due to his power and had taken out every single pursuer who came after him—but even in Academy City, the headquarters of the science world, he remained undefeated.

Suddenly, a voice called out.

"This is… This is crazy. Freaking crazy."

A short distance away from the encirclement of crumpled girls stood another person, a young man. Gunha Sogiita—number seven.

Academy City's seventh-ranked Level Five and a man with more than an appreciation for passion and guts.

He made a disgusted face at the scene before him.

But not at the fact that nine girls existed who all had the same face. Sogiita didn't care one bit about trivial mysteries like that.

"…Standing there like you're delighted to have beaten these delicate little, er… nonuplets, I guess, to a pulp? You're crazy. This is the first time I've seen such an insane lack of *guts*."

"There's a good reason for this, you know," said Ollerus with a chuckle. Slowly, he brought his head around to look at Number Seven.

"If Academy City wishes to recover the fifty or so Uncut Gems throughout the world," he continued, "then I will not stop that. But I cannot ignore the risk that they might simply become the subjects of who knows what research right here within the city walls."

As the city was gathering them here using irregular methods, they—the Uncut Gems—would naturally catch the attention of the local scientists as uniquely rare and valuable resources. There was a nonzero possibility they'd wind up stuffed into some dark institution.

"That's why I've come to give them a warning," said Ollerus. "Acting as a check—or perhaps that's too vague. This is more like a negotiation using martial force. Defeating you, who is number seven in Academy City as well as the world's greatest Uncut Gem, should be enough. That will communicate my intentions to *him* should the Uncut Gems entrusted to the city be treated as disposable."

"Really?" Number Seven grinned. "That's nice. That sentiment has guts behind it. Coming to pick a fight with Academy City's dark underbelly in order to negotiate for just fifty kids? And to do that, you'd physically confront a Level Five? That's pretty great—definitely the kind of mindset that takes a *lot* of guts.

"But!" finished Sogiita with a raised finger. "You don't know who those kids are or where they're from. And yet you've still rallied your manly self and tried desperately to protect them anyway. And maybe one of those people was a complete stranger: a certain Number Seven, whom you've never even talked to in your life."

"……"

"I don't have a responsibility to risk my life or anything, but I'll use a bit of my guts here. Anyway, long story short… *This is for real.*"

A moment later, Number Seven did something very simple:

He took a determined step toward Ollerus, grabbed him by the head, and smashed him into the side of a nearby container.

But…

…what would happen if you performed those actions at twice the speed of sound?

There was a mind-boggling *bang!!*

The metal container easily crumpled, and Ollerus, after slipping out of Sogiita's hand, crashed through it and flew dozens of meters away. A cluster of containers collapsed like a house of cards. Some of them threatened to rain down on Sogiita and the fallen girls as well, but he raised a hand overhead and blew away the airborne containers like a volcano.

Thick clouds of dust shrouded them.

The only sound was the constant, irregular, eerie clattering of metal.

And then Number Seven narrowed his eyes and tsked.

"For someone so depraved, you sure do have a lot of guts, though it's still real twisted."

"No, you were right the first time—I'm a gutless person."

The voice rose from the dust. Its source formed a silhouette as Ollerus slowly walked toward him.

He hadn't changed a bit. Not even a hair on his head was out of place.

"But, well… I do have a reason. A reason to fight. Unlike you."

"……"

Number Seven couldn't rightly respond.

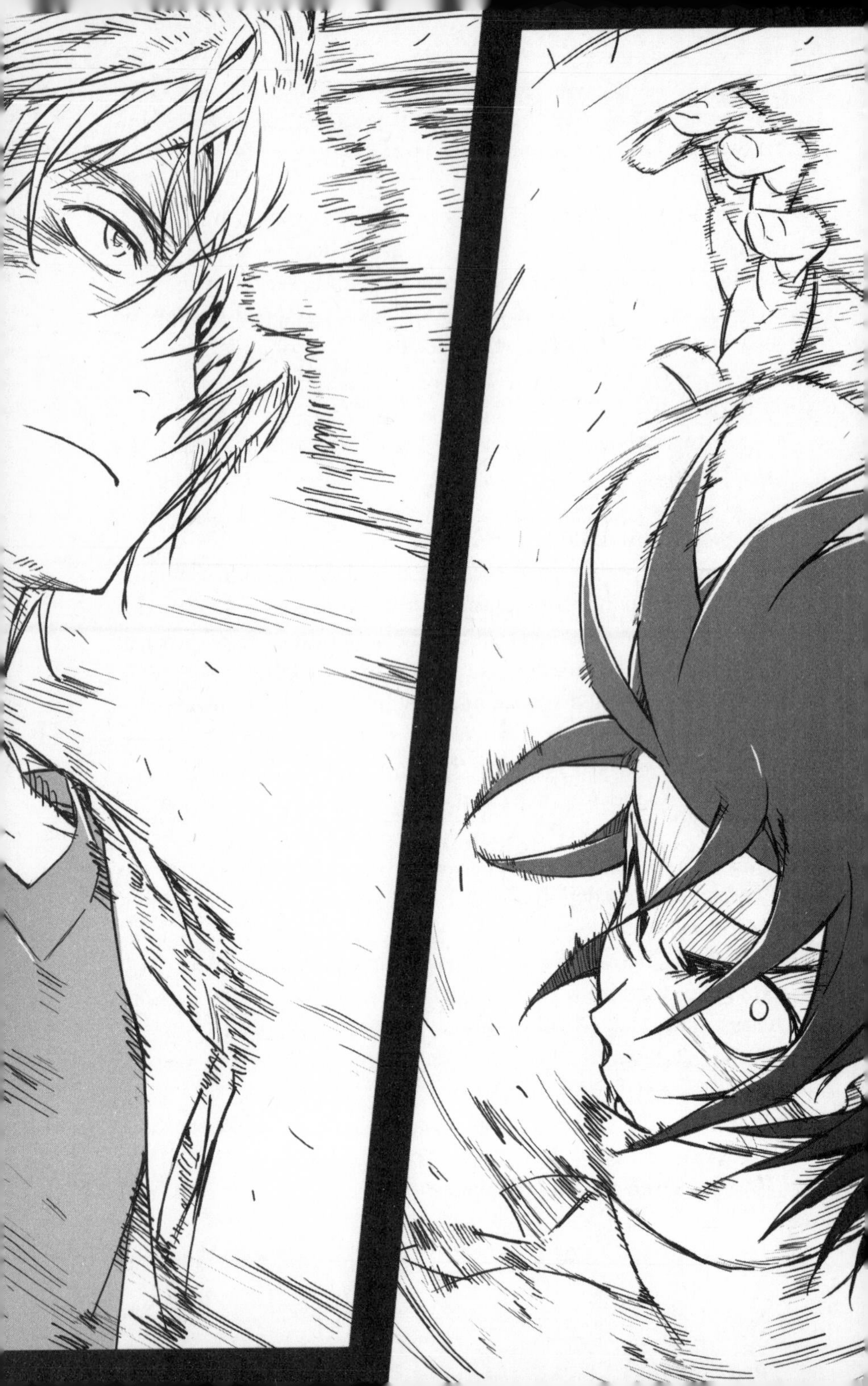

He tried approaching Ollerus to beat some guts into the guy. However…

…this time, it was Ollerus's turn to show his true power.

In short, it was an inexplicable phenomenon.

Even Sogiita, who took the attack face-first, had absolutely no idea what had just happened to him.

But the next thing he knew, his body was flying away. The damage washed over him—all of it equal, from the surface of his skin right down to the core of his body. This wasn't an attack that struck a single place, with the impact spreading through him after it hit. It was more like soaking a cloth in water. Unnatural damage was now permeating his entire body.

"……?"

Even after suffering the clean hit, his legs giving out, and his body crumpling to the ground, Sogiita wasn't afraid—he just had questions.

Ollerus's attack hadn't even allowed him to sense a threat to his life.

"The most fearsome attacks in this world come from powers that cannot be explained."

The lips of the man who should have become a magic god moved.

"No matter how vast the wellspring of mysterious power, if you swing it down like you would a sword, you need only respond in kind. If you fire it like a gun, you can defend yourself in the same way you would against a gun. That's all that 'strange attacks' are when explained on the most basic level."

Number Seven groaned as he tried to pull himself out of his prone position.

Ollerus didn't move.

He made absolutely no action that could be explained or understood.

But something *still* happened, and Sogiita's body was blown even farther away.

"But you can't deal with inexplicable powers that way."

Ollerus spoke quietly and slowly.

"The most fearsome thing in the world is to be defeated by something you cannot understand, by powers that cannot be explained, and without any time to think of a counter. The ambiguity makes it impossible to even define conditions, and it forces you to fight without knowing if dodging the attacks is possible even if you moved thousands of kilometers away in any direction. I believe you now know how frustrating such a thing can be."

There was no gasp of surprise from Sogiita.

Though it was incomplete, Ollerus *had* struck him directly with his Hliðskjálf twice. Originally, the throne that appeared in Scandinavian legend had no such offensive properties—but Ollerus's spell forcibly used it as a weapon, which was how he'd escalated its force into something inexplicable. He'd used it while keeping the attack's scope and power only vaguely defined, and Number Seven was probably already out cold.

"You and I aren't so different," he said quietly, relaxing. "One of us is subjectively wielding an inexplicable power, and the other isn't. That's about the only thing that sets us apart. The delicate and complex Number Seven, whom even Academy City's scientists couldn't meddle with... In fact, you're such a unique esper they're not even sure if they should really be classifying you as a Level Five. And if you'd understood that, you might have been able to beat me."

The goal of the man who should have become a magic god was to fight Number Seven and defeat him with overwhelming power.

It was a subtle restraint against Academy City for its collection of all those Uncut Gems.

Ollerus, deciding this show would do the trick, quietly turned around to leave.

"And I do have a reason I can't allow myself to lose, either. It might have been a disaster for you, but stay down—for your own good. This isn't about what your guts can or cannot do."

And then...

* * *

"…I can't let *that* go now, can I?"

Ollerus heard someone get up.

He slowly turned around to find the wound-covered young man standing there. By all accounts, he should have been unconscious after getting hit twice by the unknown attack Hliðskjálf, and yet he was standing. It didn't mesh with Ollerus's calculations. But this *was* the kind of world Ollerus and the others lived in.

"Don't you *dare* treat someone like they've got no guts before they've even given up, you turd."

Blood dripped from Number Seven's brow.

His breathing was ragged.

But he ignored the intense pain and glared at his opponent.

"Don't think for a second I'll go down that easy. I'll show you that strength is more than getting all cocky on your high horse…! Guts isn't something you lose just because you don't have the advantage anymore!!"

Roar!! Some sort of strange energy surrounded Sogiita.

"I'll show you what *real* guts looks like!! I don't need any outrageous reasoning. If a man walks the straight and narrow and never strays from his path, he can at the very least stand up for some wounded girls, regardless of whether they're total strangers or whatever!!"

Number Seven didn't fight it—he let the energy fill him, then began to run forward.

Unlike Ollerus's inexplicable powers, he simply ran forward.

Ollerus laughed in response.

And as he did, he made no moves that could be explained or understood.

The third cast of Hliðskjálf—and the charge of the seventh-ranked Level Five.

The indescribable, inexplicable, and incomprehensible monsters clashed.

And then…

CHAPTER 22

No One Can Reach That Ending Alone

Second Friday of October

George Kingdom broke out into a greasy, full-body sweat.

He was the actual leader (rather than the documented leader) of Stargate—the supernatural ability development enterprise a certain country had established during the Cold War. Although that enterprise had failed, he remained a powerful figure and still headed up several projects that were occasionally whispered of in rumors even in the present day. His legendary value was so high, he had free rein over the CIA.

However.

Right now, at this moment, it was all about to come crashing down.

It was strange. He was sure he'd prepared for even the most irregular possibilities, and yet the beast called reality had slipped through the cracks, carrying a terrible conclusion for him. An operation to abduct the Uncut Gems, carried out across the planet all at once. Over fifty independent organizations, each with its own funding and historical foundation, had all been crushed by *someone* before they'd gotten any results and the entire project had been destroyed.

The term *self-defense* crossed his mind.

He'd implemented this project at his own discretion, and it had not borne any fruit whatsoever—the only thing that had been accomplished was the flushing of a huge amount of resources down the drain. The Senate would not let this slide. His reputation as well as his very life were most likely forfeit.

But one thing dominated George's mind, and it overrode his terror.

What…?

A question.

The question of who, exactly, had physically foiled this project. But that wasn't because he hadn't been able to see the people who had assaulted each of the organizations. He'd received the latest reports about spies having infiltrated all operational theaters.

What happened…?

But the question was still there.

This operation had the highest degree of confidentiality. Because of that, George Kingdom was the only one who could unify all that information. And thus, he was the *only* one who had this question out of all those who were involved.

Why?

Why had a bunch of girls, all with the same face, launched attacks across the entire world simultaneously?

Then, George heard a short static buzz by his ear. He'd only shared his radio frequency with his aides, and they'd all supposedly been defeated in the aforementioned attacks.

"Done putting your affairs in order?" came the voice of the General Board's brain. *"Conclusions without trials are underhanded. And as someone who stands in the shadows yourself, I expect you know what it means to make an entire country your enemy."*

"Kumokawa…" George was baffled. Forgetting even his anger, he asked, "Was that…? Did you…? The mass-produced…"

"Oh, yes. And about that," confirmed the girl genius Seria Kumokawa in a lighthearted tone. *"Creating humans using somatic cells is technically forbidden by international law, and we're quite reluctant to put those girls in harm's way for military operations like today. I figured, since you owed us, we'd at least provide you with ample amounts of aftercare."*

"……"

George Kingdom was now certain of one thing:

He'd set foot into a place he never should have ventured into.

He currently stood in a special facility that could function as a shelter if needed, but that didn't give him any peace of mind. Ever since ancient times, those foolish enough to get involved where they shouldn't had but one fate.

Click.

It was a soft footstep.

"Great... I finally got to make my triumphant return, and now I have to deal with this super-greasy old man who just doesn't get how things work? Oh well, guess I'll go see some movies after this job is over or something. Might as well make it, like, a big festival of super-obscure ones not released in Japan."

A girl's voice.

George Kingdom couldn't turn around.

By the time his brain relayed the commands to his neck, it was all over.

Gunha Sogiita, number seven, lay beaten on the ground, faceup, his wound-covered body exposed.

Above him, he had an unobscured view of a wide-open starry sky.

Everything around him was a total disaster now; it was like the area itself wanted to show off the scars it had from a fierce battle. Piles of containers lay broken and scattered; chunks of asphalt had been flipped over; and in places, the very foundation of the ground had cracked, the edges swelling upward to form cliffs.

And yet, even then, he hadn't been able to win.

The man who said during the battle that he was supposed to become a magic god had bested Sogiita.

Crazy..., he thought.

Despite having been beaten down with overwhelming power, there was a pure light in his eyes. It was hope. The world was still crawling with insane monsters, filled with things he didn't understand. Those were Number Seven's honest impressions. It was so obvious, but the world really was a big place.

This planet is brimming with crazy, awesome people.

This time, Number Seven was no match. That man who should have become a magic god had probably been holding back, too. He knew when he was being toyed with. He'd challenged the man with his full power; been treated as though he were a plaything; and then, to add insult to injury, had been left alive.

His opponent had been overwhelming.

Sogiita knew that much for sure. Eventually, slowly, he got to his feet.

The way he did it was like someone waking up from a short afternoon nap.

Without any hurry, he raised his hands above him and stretched. Then his lips moved, and he spoke.

"All righty, then... Gotta get my guts back in tip-top shape. Time for some new training."

The road—if you could even call it that—seemed to go on forever in this part of the Arizonan desert.

An off-roader was parked on it, with a man sitting on the car's hood and holding a cell phone to his ear.

Tabigake Misaka.

He made his livelihood guiding the world in a better direction without relying on violence pointing out what it was the world lacked.

"I mean, it kind of seems like a bunch of troubling stuff happened."

"Same chaos as usual. Not the kind of thing you'd be part of."

"I'm sure. *I* certainly wouldn't use these sorts of methods. I came up with three more peaceful options over the course of the last couple sentences alone."

"It's a cost issue. Depends on the situation, but in this case, it was less expensive to wrap it all up with a fight."

"Can't get behind that." Misaka sighed, then picked up the cup of coffee sitting on the hood. "Still, this means those slim possibilities scattered throughout the world are all being recovered and sent to Academy City at once. We already had no clues about them, but this'll completely cut them off from any hints that would lead to successful supernatural ability development. Truly something only *you* could have accomplished."

He took a sip of the bitter liquid and grinned.

"By the way, there's something I wanted to confirm about this little quarrel."

"*What?*"

"I mean, the market seems to be a mess now, too, and I'm just confirming because the people I heard from aren't very trustworthy. That is, well, Academy City is a city of espers. It's always *possible* that someone can use the shadow clone technique, and it's *possible* there's some kind of monster who can instantly teleport tens of thousands of kilometers, but still…"

"……"

"Well, I'm talking about how girls with the exact same face were spotted at those fifty or so research organizations scattered throughout the world."

Misaka's tone of voice shifted.

It wasn't an extreme change, like a wave of emotion had come over him. But something had definitely changed.

"Like I said before, I can't rely on eyewitness testimony. And Academy City *is* a city of espers. Something could happen that *seems* contradictory, but all you'd have to say is that there's actually some special ability that can overcome that contradiction, and that would be the end of it."

"*I'll leave that to your imagination. I will, at least, tell you that it's not an issue you would need to be worried about.*"

"I see," said Misaka casually. And then he asked, "Then the intel that said that the traits of these girls who were seen are extremely similar to my own daughter's isn't a problem I need to worry about, is it?"

"*…Hmm.*"

"Look, Aleister, if you say so, then I don't really mind. I can't trust what you say to begin with. But just remember one thing. If I ever hear that you actually did anything to my wife or daughter... Well, you might want to think, at least a little, about what would happen if you made an enemy out of this worthless father."

"How would you do it?"

The owner of the voice, called Aleister, came back with a simple question.

"How would a single freelancer attack the chairman of Academy City's General Board?"

"Sure, maybe there's nothing I could do to take you out in one hit with the way the world is set up."

Misaka acknowledged that fact.

But he added anyway:

"My job is simply to show the world what it lacks. If something's missing, it *is* my business. That's why I warned you to remember that one thing."

The adults' conversation ended.

After their disquieting exchange, both of them slipped back into the underbelly of the world.

Sylvia was vacuuming the hallway in her apartment.

Most of the children brought here by some idiot or another had been entrusted to the Church—and from what she'd heard, many had been taken in by new foster parents to start their second lives—but several were still in the apartment. They weren't the left-overs who couldn't find new homes—they'd remained because they *wanted* to wait for the return of some idiot or another.

She sighed.

What was she still doing in a place like this? Her long-term over-seas in-service training period meant to polish her skills as a *bonne dame* had already ended, and she'd gotten repeated orders to go back home to the United Kingdom. She wasn't exactly drawing a proper salary to begin with, and this wasn't one of those old tra-ditional master-servant relationships, either. She made her own money to live off, so she hardly had any reasons to feel tied down to this apartment. Now that the idiot had set off on his own, there was no point in her staying anymore. Going back to the UK that very instant or moving to a better location would have both been better options, but for some reason, she just couldn't bring herself to leave this apartment.

Well, all reasons tended to be silly.

It would have been utterly ridiculous to even put it into words.

When Sylvia sighed again, she spotted something outside the window. She scratched her hair in disinterest, then set the vacuum down and headed for the front door. Same as always, she opened it—and same as always, she said:

"Yo—welcome back, you massive idiot."

AFTERWORD

For those who have been reading through one book at a time, it's good to see you again.

For those who read through everything at once, it's a pleasure to meet you.

I'm Kazuma Kamachi.

And this is the second short-story volume!! I tried to write this one in a way so you could, to an extent, understand the vignettes without having read the main story. How did it turn out? I personally think I was able to express this world from a whole bunch of different angles: the sorcery side, the science side, and even the normal people's side.

The overall theme is "time is long," and the key term is *Uncut Gem*, I suppose.

And surprise! This book alone covers almost a year.

This is the second short-story volume, but the story of the Uncut Gems started and finished in it. I'm sure some of you who read to the end may be thinking *huh?* Like, did it really get resolved? Or that one person didn't end up getting retrieved—what happened to them? Your hunches are correct—in this second short-story volume, which revolves around the Uncut Gems, there are actually other, unmentioned things the story also revolves around. You may find it interesting to come up with theories for this or that.

*   *   *

Oh, right. In regard to the two superstrong characters who appeared, both of them are the sort that break all the rules in this kind of battle. As for why—well, there's zero set procedure for their battles. Though perhaps things could have been resolved more forcibly, like with a giant frontal blast that was even stronger than the full might of that inexplicable power.

Speaking of unusual characters, not one but *two* ninjas show up. In this world, that is what their methods and goals are like. These ninjas are less a formal occupation, like the samurai, and more a way of thinking and acting; the story this time was about the dissension about how it's carried out. It might be interesting to dig into their story some more, but they both have to obey the ironic rule of finding significance in devoting themselves to being side characters, so leaving it at that is probably for the best. In a way, they're buried even farther underground than sorcerers are.

Actually, I personally think the *strongest* one in this book was Daddy Misaka. What did you think of him? He, again, is someone with a different methodology than those in the main *Index* story in that he changes the world through methods that don't involve people killing each other. But it's not that he doesn't fight, just that he fights differently. He's not the kind of saint who would reject fighting altogether. And since he interferes with the foundations and cornerstones of societies, that fact might make him all the more dangerous than the children who only know how to swing their fists and punch it out.

Technically, Touya Kamijou is able to oppose Daddy Misaka. Dandy gentlemen have their own battles to fight. Though they both experience a bit of hardship, with one getting pushed around by subordinates and being a corporate warrior late to be promoted while the other's wallet is being tightly managed by his wife.

...Actually, when I look at just the two short-story volumes, I'm astonished at the utter lack of connection between them. The only thin threads are the parts surrounding Skill-Out's destruction. Short-story "series"? Yeah, right. Still, it's more fun to purposely rip out all the demarcations and definitions and make this into an experiment where anything goes. If a third volume ever comes out, it'll probably be even *less* connected to the others.

I'd like to thank my illustrator, Haimura, and my editor, Miki. Things got rough with the stage changing so many times and with there being so many chapters, but thank you for sticking with me through it all anyway.

And I want to thank all my readers. These short-story volumes started with the simple idea that things should begin and end in a single volume and then breaking that apart a little. Thank you for reading them.

Now then, as you close the pages here,
and as I pray that you will open the front page of the next volume as well,
today, at this hour, I lay down my pen.

Hey, why's so much stuff happening without Kamijou knowing?
Kazuma Kamachi

Volume 2 has been published already, huh? Ooohhh... Incredible!!

So many new characters! This will probably be another indispensable volume for depicting the Index world!

The theme was characters I've never drawn, so I decided on Itsuwa, who has been skyrocketing in popularity.

Chuya Kogino

CONGRATULATIONS ON THE RELEASE OF SS2!

SS... This is the second story told from an angle the main story can't tell.

Aside from my questions related to Railgun, I frequently ask Mr. Kamachi about things on my mind (like how do the Sisters, who aren't Tokiwadai students, have the same uniform), knowing they're a nuisance, but every time, he goes into very specific background details.

It always surprises me.

I only know a small fragment of everything, but there are still plenty of interesting stories to be told in *Index*!

If they were all made into short-story volumes, there would end up being a crazy number of them.

............I'm rooting for you, Haimura.

Motoi
Fuyukawa

冬川基

TRANSLATOR'S AFTERWORD

Hello everyone. I'm Andrew Prowse, the translator for the *A Certain Magical Index* novels. With the so-called Old Testament arc complete at last, I managed to talk the good folks at Yen Press into letting me write an additional afterword as a little bonus for the readers! It isn't much, but please enjoy this brief pulling back of the curtain before I return to my perch behind the scenes.

Despite having done hobby translation for a while in the past, this series was my first-ever professional translation project, and boy, was it a rude awakening. The first few volumes were a trial by fire for me, but thanks to the help of several kind, helpful editors, I managed to pull through. Part of me never thought I'd keep going for six years, and I'm glad I did. I feel like I've grown as a translator so much since then—both in my understanding of the Japanese language and in my personal writing skills.

Before starting on this project, I had only very cursory knowledge of *A Certain Magical Index* and its spin-off series, but the stars aligned: After reading some of it, I realized I enjoyed it quite a bit. And that enjoyment only grew the further into the series we progressed. I can only pray I've done it justice for all the Western fans out there, because I now count myself among your number!

There is so much I could talk about when it comes to my translation decisions for this series, including regarding terminology choices—and specifically, the names of the religions. While I don't have much room to talk about them here, I'd like to note that the author's terms for these religions are not what the real-world ones are called in Japan, but shorter, custom-made ones, presumably made to be more readable to a Japanese audience. (This may be why it sounds a bit strange to Western readers.)

And don't even get me *started* on the *kami-jo* bit. Talk about impossible translations! I think the way that I rendered it worked out, but—just wow. That level of pun on the main character's name coming so late in the series was an absolute shocker...

I could talk about translation forever, but time is short and space is at a premium, so I'd like to use the rest to give a few shout-outs. First, to the various Internet resources out there dedicated to cataloging everything there is to know about the *Index*-verse. Without that extensive information being readily available, certain references may have gone straight over my head, so I wanted to make sure to thank the entire *Index* community, both in Japan and in the Western world. (I'd also like to shout out a Russian friend of mine for helping me with the spellings of a few minor character names in the World War III arc. Thanks, Arknarok!)

I'd like to thank my editors for giving me a shot at such a monumental project. I think, ultimately, we succeeded in bringing this light novel behemoth to the English-speaking world in a way that did it justice. It's hard to believe this long project is at an end, but for the time being, I will still be working on the official manga adaptation!

Finally, I want to thank the original creator, Kazuma Kamachi. This series has done far more for me than just pay the bills. It's helped me grow as a reader, a translator, and a person. It's given me enjoyment on long car rides trying to explain the lore of the *Index* world to my friends; it's given me something to look forward to between projects; it's given me a chance to improve my craft.

Most of all, though, it's given me something to be proud of.

With that, I lay down my own pen...
...or close my laptop, as it were. Not quite the same ring to it, eh?

See you again next time,
Andrew Prowse